The Day's Play

by

A. A. Milne

Double 9
BOOKS

The Day's Play
by A. A. Milne

ISBN: 978-93-61151-48-4

Published by

DOUBLE 9 BOOKS

2/13-B, Ansari Road
Daryaganj, New Delhi – 110002
info@double9books.com
www.double9books.com
Tel. 011-40042856

ABOUT THE AUTHOR

Alan Alexander Milne was an English author best known for his books about the teddy bear Winnie-the-Pooh and for children's poetry. Milne was primarily a dramatist before the enormous popularity of Winnie-the-Pooh eclipsed all of his earlier work. Milne fought in both World Wars, as a lieutenant in the Royal Warwickshire Regiment in WWI and a captain in the Home Guard in WWII. Alan Alexander Milne was born in Kilburn, London, on January 18, 1882, to Jamaican-born John Vine Milne and Sarah Marie Milne. He was raised at Henley House School, 6/7 Mortimer Road (now Crescent), Kilburn, a small independent school owned by his father. H. G. Wells was one of his teachers from 1889 to 1890. Milne attended Westminster School and Trinity College, Cambridge, where he received a mathematics scholarship and graduated with a B.A. in Mathematics in 1903. He edited and wrote for Granta, a student publication. He cooperated with his brother Kenneth on articles that appeared under the letters AKM.

CONTENTS

THE RABBITS

PART I

CHAPTER I
INTRODUCING THE LOP-EARED
ONES AND OTHERS

"By Hobbs," cried Archie, as he began to put away the porridge, "I feel as fit as anything this morning. I'm absolutely safe for a century."

"You shouldn't boast with your mouth full," Myra told her brother.

"It wasn't quite full," pleaded Archie, "and I really am good for runs to-day."

"You will make," I said, "exactly fourteen."

"Hallo, good-morning. Didn't see you were there."

"I have been here all the time. Fourteen."

"It seems a lot," said Myra doubtfully.

Archie laughed in scorn.

"The incoming batsman," I began, "who seemed in no way daunted by the position of affairs ——"

"Five hundred for nine," put in Myra.

"—reached double figures for the fourth time this season, with a lofty snick to the boundary. Then turning his attention to the slow bowler he despatched him between his pads and the wicket for a couple. This, however, was his last scoring stroke, as in the same over he played forward to a long hop and fell a victim to the vigilance of the wicket-keeper."

"For nearly a quarter of an hour," continued Myra, "he had defied the attack, and the character of his batting may be easily judged from the fact that his score included one five ——"

"Four from an overthrow," I added in parenthesis.

"And one four. Save for a chance to mid-on before he had scored, and another in the slips when seven, his innings was almost entirely free from blemish— —"

"Although on one occasion he had the good fortune, when playing back to a half-volley, to strike the wicket without dislodging the bails."

"See to-morrow's *Sportsman*," concluded Myra.

"Oh, you children," laughed Archie, as he walked over to inspect the ham. "Bless you."

Miss Fortescue gave a little cough and began to speak. Miss Fortescue is one of those thoroughly good girls who take an interest in everything. A genuine trier. On this occasion she said: "I often wonder who it is who writes those accounts in *The Sportsman*."

"It is believed to be Mr Simpson," said Archie.

Simpson looked up with a start, and jerked his glasses into his tea. He fished them out and wiped them thoughtfully.

"The credible," he began, "is rarely— —"

"Gentlemen, I pray you silence for Mr Simpson's epigram," cried Archie.

"Oh, I always thought Mr Simpson wrote verses in *The Saturday Review*," said Miss Fortescue in the silence which followed.

"As a relaxation only," I explained. "The other is his life-work. We read him with great interest; that bit about the heavy roller being requisitioned is my favourite line."

"Mr Simpson and Killick and Crawford all play in glasses," put in Myra eagerly, across the table.

"That is their only point in common," added Archie.

"Oh, isn't he a very good player?"

"Well, he's a thoroughly honest and punctual and sober player," I said, "but—the fact is, he and I and the Major don't make many runs nowadays. We generally give, as he has said in one of his less popular poems, a local habitation to the—er—airy nothing."

"I thought it was Shakespeare said that."

"Shakespeare or Simpson. Hallo, there's Thomas at last."

Thomas is in the Admiralty, which is why he is always late. It is a great pity that he was christened Thomas; he can never rise to the top of his profession with a name like that. You couldn't imagine a Thomas McKenna—or even a Thomas Nelson, but he doesn't seem to mind somehow.

"Morning, everybody," said Thomas. "Isn't it a beastly day?"

"We'll hoist the south cone for you," said Archie, and he balanced a mushroom upside down on the end of his fork.

"What's the matter with the day?" asked our host, the Major, still intent on his paper.

"It's so early."

"When I was a boy——"

"My father, Major Mannering," said Archie, "will now relate an anecdote of Waterloo."

But the Major was deep in his paper. Suddenly he—there is only one word for it—snorted.

"The Budget," said Myra and Archie, exchanging anxious glances.

"Ha, that's good," he said, "that's very good! 'If the Chancellor of the Exchequer imagines that he can make his iniquitous Budget more acceptable to a disgusted public by treating it in a spirit of airy persiflage he is at liberty to try. But airy persiflage, when brought into contact with the determined temper of a nation——'"

"Who is the hairy Percy, anyhow?" said Thomas to himself.

The Major glared at the interrupter for a moment. Then—for he knows his weakness, and is particularly fond of Thomas—he threw his paper down and laughed. "Well," he said, "are we going to win to-day?" And while he and Archie talked about the wicket his daughter removed *The Times* to a safe distance.

"But there aren't eleven of you, here," said Miss Fortescue to me, "and if you and Mr Simpson and Major Mannering aren't very good you'll be beaten. It's against the village the first two days, isn't it?"

"When I said we weren't very good, I only meant we didn't make many runs. Mr Simpson is a noted fast bowler, the Major has a M.C.C. scarf, which can be seen quite easily at point, and I keep wicket. Between us we dismiss many a professor. Just as they are shaping for a cut, you know, they catch sight of the Major's scarf, lose their heads and give me an easy catch. Then Archie and Thomas take centuries, one of the gardeners bends them from the off and makes them swim a bit, the Vicar of his plenty is lending us two sons, Tony and Dahlia Blair come down this morning, and there is a chauffeur who plays for keeps. How many is that?"

"Eleven, isn't it?"

"It ought only to be ten," said Myra, who had overheard.

"Oh yes, I was counting Miss Blair," said Miss Fortescue.

"We never play more than ten a side," said Archie.

"Oh, why?"

"So as to give the scorer an extra line or two for the byes."

Myra laughed; then, catching my eye, looked preternaturally solemn.

"If you've quite finished breakfast, Mr Gaukrodger," she said, "there'll be just time for me to beat you at croquet before the Rabbits take the field."

"Right O," I said.

Of course, you know, my name isn't really Gaukrodger.

CHAPTER II
ON THE RUN

The Major has taken a great deal of trouble with his ground, and the result pleases everybody. If you are a batsman you applaud the short boundaries; if you are a wicket-keeper (as I am), and Thomas is bowling what he is pleased to call googlies, you have leisure to study some delightful scenery; and if you are a left-handed bowler, with a delivery outside the screen, there is behind you a belt of trees which you cannot fail to admire. When Archie was born, and they announced the fact to the Major, his first question was (so I understand), "Right or left handed?" They told him "Left" to quiet him, and he went out and planted a small forest, so that it should be ready for Archibald's action when he grew up. Unfortunately, Archie turned out to be no bowler at all (in my opinion)—and right-handed at that. Nemesis, as the ha'penny papers say.

"Well?" we all asked, when Archie came back from tossing.

"They lost, and put us in."

"Good man."

"May I have my sixpence back?" I said. "You haven't bent it or anything, have you? Thanks."

As the whole pavilion seemed to be full of people putting on their pads in order to go in first, I wandered outside. There I met Myra.

"Hallo, we're in," I said. "Come and sit on the roller with me, and I'll tell you all about Jayes."

"Can't for a moment. Do go and make yourself pleasant to Dahlia Blair. She's just come."

"Do you think she'd be interested in Jayes? I mean the Leicestershire cricketer, not the disinfectant. Oh, all right, then, I won't."

I wandered over to the deck-chairs, and exchanged greetings with Miss Blair.

"I have been asked to make myself pleasant," I said. "I suppose that means telling you all about everybody, doesn't it?"

"Yes, please."

"Well, we're in, as you see. That's the Vicar leading his team out. He's no player really—one of the 'among others we noticed.' But he's a good father, and we've borrowed two offsprings from him. Here comes Archie and Wilks. Wilks drove you from the station, I expect?"

"He did. And very furiously."

"Well, he hardly drives at all, when he's in. He's terribly slow—what they call Nature's reaction. Archie, you will be sorry to hear, has just distinguished himself by putting me in last. He called it ninth wicket down, but I worked it out, and there doesn't seem to be anybody after me. It's simply spite."

"I hope Mr Archie makes some runs," said Dahlia. "I don't mind so much about Wilks, you know."

"I'm afraid he is only going to make fourteen to-day. That's the postman going to bowl to him. He has two deliveries, one at eight A.M. and one at twelve-thirty P.M.—the second one is rather doubtful. Archie always takes guard with the bail, you observe, and then looks round to see if we're all watching."

"Don't be so unkind."

"I'm annoyed," I said, "and I intensely dislike the name Archibald. Ninth wicket down!"

The umpire having called "Play," Joe, the postman, bounded up to the wicket and delivered the ball. Archie played forward with the easy confidence of a school professional when nobody is bowling to him. And then the leg-bail disappeared.

"Oh!" cried Dahlia. "He's out!"

I looked at her, and I looked at Archie's disconsolate back as he made for the pavilion; and I knew what he would want. I got up.

"I must go now," I said. "I've promised to sit on the heavy roller for a bit. Archie will be here in a moment. Will you tell him from me that we both thought he wasn't quite ready for that one, and that it never rose an inch? Thank you very much."

I discovered Myra, and we sat on the roller together.

"Well, I've been making myself pleasant," I said. "And then when Archie got out I knew he'd want to sit next to her, so I came away. That is what they call tact in *The Lady*."

"Archie is rather fond of her," said Myra. "I don't know if——"

"Yes, yes, I understand. Years ago——"

"Let's see. Are you ninety or ninety-one? I always forget."

"Ninety-one next St Crispin's Day. I'm sorry Archie's out. 'The popular cricketer was unfortunate enough to meet a trimmer first ball, and the silent sympathy of the Bank Holiday crowd went out to him as he wended his way to the Pavilion.' Extract from 'Pavilions I have wended to, by Percy Benskin.' Help! There goes Blair!"

After this the situation became very serious. In an hour seven of us had got what I might call the postman's knock. Wilks was still in, but he had only made nine. The score was fifty-two, thanks entirely to Simpson, who had got thirty-five between first and second slip in twenty minutes. This stroke of his is known as the Simpson upper cut, and is delivered straight from the shoulder and off the edge of the bat.

"This is awful," said Myra. "You'll simply have to make some now."

"I think it's time Wilks got on to his second speed. Why doesn't somebody tell him? Hallo, there goes John. I knew there wasn't a run there. Where are my gloves?"

"You mustn't be nervous. Oh, do make some."

"The condemned man walked firmly to the wickets. 'What is that, umpire?' he asked in his usual cool voice. 'Houtside the leg stump, sir,' said the man in white. 'Good,' he replied.... What an ass your second gardener is. Fancy being potted out like that, just as if he were a geranium. I ought to wear a cap, oughtn't I, in case I want to bow when I come in. Good-bye; I shall be back for lunch, I expect."

I passed Joe on my way to the wickets, and asked pleasantly after his wife and family. He was rather brusque about it, and sent down a very fast half-volley which kept low. Then Wilks and I returned to the pavilion together amid cheers. On the whole, the Rabbits had lived up to their reputation.

"Well, we are a lot of bunnies," said Archie at lunch. "Joe simply stands there looking like a lettuce and out we all trot. We shall have to take to halma or something. Simpson, you swim, don't you?"

"You don't have to swim at halma," said Simpson.

"Anyhow," said Blair, "we can't blame the Selection Committee."

"I blame Thomas," I said. "He would have eight, and he wouldn't wait. I don't blame myself, because my average is now three spot five, and yesterday it was only three spot one."

"That is impossible, if you made nought to-day," said Simpson eagerly.

"Not if I divided it wrong yesterday."

"Averages," said the Major to the Vicar, catching the last sentence but two, "are the curse of modern cricket. When I was a boy— —"

"This," Archie explained to us, "takes us back to the thirties, when Felix Mynn bowled Ensign Mannering with a full pilch."

"Dear old Fuller Pilch. Ah! what do they know of England, who only King and Jayes?" I declaimed. "Libretto by Simpson."

"Who's finished?" said Archie, getting up. "Come out and smoke. Now, we simply must buck up and out the opposition. Simpson ought to bump them at Joe's end, and Thomas— —"

"I always swerve after lunch," said Thomas.

"I don't wonder. What I was going to say was that you would box them in the slips. You know, if we all buck up— —"

We bucked up and outed them by the end of the day for two hundred and fifty.

CHAPTER III
GOOD SHOOTING

"Will somebody give me a cigarette," said Myra, stretching out a hand.

"I fancy not," I said. "Thomas and I both feel that you are too young."

"I don't really want one, but when I'm locked up in the billiard-room with two dumb men— —"

"We were reflecting on our blessed victory."

"Were you thinking of Archie's century or John's bowling?"

"Neither, oddly enough. I was recalling my own catch which won the match. Poetry; let's go and tell Simpson."

"It was a skier," said Myra. "I thought it was never coming down. What did you think of all the time?"

"Everything. All my past life flashed before my eyes. I saw again my happy childhood's days, when I played innocently in the—er—pantry. I saw myself at school, sl—working. I saw— —"

"Did you happen," interrupted Thomas, when we both thought he was fast asleep, "to see yourself being badly taken on by me at billiards?"

"Thomas, you're not properly awake, old friend. I know that feeling. Turn over on the other side and take a deep breath."

Thomas rose and stretched himself, and went over to the cue rack. "You should have heard him siding about his blessed billiards this morning," he told Myra.

"I didn't side. I simply said that anybody could beat Thomas. Do they play billiards much at the Admiralty? I should have thought the motion— —"

"Take a cue. Myra will mark."

"Rather; I can mark like anything."

"Once upon a time," I said, "there was a lad who wanted to get into the Admiralty. But his mother said, 'Not until you have learnt to swim, Thomas.' So he had a set of six private lessons for one guinea before he went in for the examination. He came out thirty-eight, and was offered a lucrative appointment in the post office.... Hence his enormous skill at billiards. Thick or clear?"

"I will adventure half-a-crown upon the game," said Thomas, giving a miss.

"Right O, Rothschild. Now, are you ready, marker? I'm spot. Hadn't you better oil the board a bit? Well, as long as you can work it quickly enough."

I took careful aim, and my ball went up the table and back again, with the idea, I imagine, of inspecting the wicket. It seemed quite fast.

"One all," said Myra, and Thomas kindly brought his ball and mine to the top of the table.

"I fancy I shall be able to swerve from this end," I said. I tried a delicate cannon, and just missed the object ball. "I shall find a spot directly—there's one under the red ball, I believe."

"Do try and hit something," said Myra.

"The marker is not allowed to give advice," I said sternly. "What's the matter, Thomas?"

"I'm not quite sure what to do."

"I think you ought to chalk your cue here," I said, after examining the position.

"I've done that."

"Then ram the red."

Thomas rammed and all but sank it in the left-hand pocket.

"I am now," I said, "going to do a cannon off the cushion. Marker, what is my score?"

"One, sir."

"Then kindly get ready to put it up to three.... Rotten luck."

"Wrong side," said Myra judicially.

"No, I meant to hit it that side."

"I mean you wanted a little running side."

"This isn't Queen's Club. Go on, Thomas."

Thomas, who had been chalking his cue, advanced to the table. "Hallo," he said, "where's the other ball?"

I looked at the table, and there were only two balls on it!

"That's an extraordinary thing," I said in amazement. "I'm almost certain we started with three."

"Did you put me down?"

"Certainly not; I shouldn't dream of doing such a thing. I don't say I mayn't have slipped down myself when nobody was looking. Myra, did you notice which pocket I was trying for that time?"

We felt in all of them, and at last found my ball in one of the bottom ones. It must have gone there very quietly.

"Score, marker?" I asked confidently, as I prepared to continue my break.

"Oh, you're going over the crease," cried Myra.

I took my ball back an inch. "*Will* you tell me the score?" I said.

"Stevenson (in play) three; Inman, two. Inman's two were both wides."

Barely were the words out of her mouth when Inman's score was increased by a no-ball. A miss-cue they call it technically.

"Three all," said Myra. "This is awfully exciting. First one is ahead, and then the other."

"By the way, how many up are we playing?"

"Five, aren't you?" said Myra.

This roused Thomas. He had played himself in, and now proceeded to make a pretty break of seventeen. I followed. There was a collision off the middle pocket between spot and red, and both went down. Then plain was unintentionally sunk as the result of a cannon shot, and spot and red sailed into harbour. With Thomas's miss I scored eleven. Unfortunately, off my next stroke, Thomas again went down.

"Billiards," he said.

"You don't think I want to put the rotten thing down, do you? It's such a blessed rabbit. Directly it sees a hole anywhere it makes for it. Hallo, six more. I shall now give what they call a miss in baulk."

"Oh, good miss," cried Myra, as spot rested over the middle pocket.

"That was a googly. You both thought it would break the other way."

The game went on slowly. When Thomas was ninety and I was ninety-nine, there was a confused noise without, and Archie and Miss Blair burst into the room. At least only Archie actually burst; Miss Blair entered sedately.

"Who's winning?" cried Archie.

"What an absurd question," I said. "As if we should tell you."

"All right. Dahl—Miss Blair, have you ever seen billiards played really well?"

"Never."

"Then now's your chance. Ninety, ninety-nine—they've only just begun. This is Thomas's first break, I expect. There—he's got a clear board. You get five extra for that, and the other man is rubiconed. Ninety-nine all. Now, it is only a question of who misses first."

I put down my cue.

"Thomas," I began, "we have said some hard things about each other to-night, but when I listen to Archie I feel very friendly towards you."

"Archibald," said Thomas, "is a beastly name."

"So I told Miss Blair. For a man who was, so to speak, born with a silver billiard-table in his mouth to come here and make fun of two persevering and, in my case, promising players, is——"

"You'll never finish that sentence," said Myra. "Try some more billiards."

"It was almost impossible to say what I wanted to say grammatically," I answered, and I hit my ball very hard up the table at the white.

"It's working across," said Archie, after the second bounce; "it must hit the red soon. I give it three more laps."

"It's going much more slowly now," said Miss Blair.

"Probably it's keeping a bit of a sprint for the finish. Wait till it gets its second wind. No, I'm afraid it's no good; it ought to have started sooner. Hallo, yes, it's—— Got him!"

"It hasn't finished yet," I said calmly. "Look—there!"

"Jove!" said Archie, shaking my hand, "that's the longest loser I've ever seen. My dear old man, what a performer. The practice you must have had. The years you must have devoted to the game. I wonder—could you *possibly* spare an hour or two to-morrow to play cricket for us?"

CHAPTER IV
A FEW WIRES

A hundred and eighty for none. The umpire waved his lily hand, and the scorer entered one more "four" in his book. Seeing that the ball had gone right through a bicycle which was leaning up against the pavilion, many people (the owner of the bicycle, anyhow) must have felt that the actual signalling of a boundary was unnecessary; but our umpire is a stickler for the etiquette of the game. Once when— — But no, on second thoughts, I sha'n't tell you that story. You would say it was a lie—as indeed it is.

"Rotten," said Archie to me, as we crossed over. (A good captain always confides in his wicket-keeper.)

"Don't take Simpson off," I said. "I like watching him."

"I shall go on again myself soon."

"Oh, it's not so bad as that. Don't lose heart."

The score was two hundred when we met again.

"I once read a book by a lady," I said, "in which the hero started the over with his right hand and finished it with his left. I suppose Simpson couldn't do that?"

"He's a darned rotten bowler, anyway."

"His direction is all right, but his metre is so irregular."

At the end of the next over, "What shall I do?" asked Archie in despair.

"Put the wicket-keeper on," I said at once.

The idea was quite a new one to him. He considered it for a moment.

"Can you bowl?" he said at last.

"No."

"Then what on earth— —"

"Look here; you've tried 'em with people who can bowl, and they've made two hundred and twenty in an hour and a half; somebody who can't bowl will be a little change for them. That's one reason. The second is that we shall all have a bit of a rest while I'm taking my things off. The third is that I bet Myra a shilling — — "

Archie knelt down, and began to unbuckle my pads. "I'll 'keep' myself," he said. "Are you fast or slow?"

"I haven't the faintest idea. Just as it occurs to me at the moment, I expect."

"Well, you're quite right; you can't be worse than some of us. Will you have a few balls down first?"

"No, thanks; I should like to come as a surprise to them."

"Well, pitch 'em up anyhow."

"I shall probably vary my length — if possible without any alteration of action."

I am now approaching the incredible. The gentle reader, however, must not be nasty about it; he should at least pretend to believe, and his best way of doing this is to listen very silently to what follows. When he has heard my explanation I shall assume that he understands.

Bowling is entirely a question of when you let go of the ball. If you let go too soon the result is a wide over the batsman's head; if too late, a nasty crack on your own foot. Obviously there are spaces in between. By the law of averages one must let go at the right moment at least once. Why not then at the first ball? And in the case of a person like myself, who has a very high action and a good mouth — I mean who has a very high delivery, such a ball (after a week of Simpsons and Archies) would be almost unplayable.

Very well then; I did let go at the right moment, but, unfortunately, I took off from the wrong crease. The umpire's cry of "No-ball" and the shattering of the Quidnunc's wicket occurred simultaneously.

"Good ball," said Archie. "Oh, bad luck!"

I tried to look as though, on the whole, I preferred it that way — as being ultimately more likely to inspire terror in the batsman at my end. Certainly, it gave me confidence; made me over-confident in fact, so that I held on to the next ball much too long, and it started bouncing almost at once.

The Quidnunc, who was convinced by this that he had been merely having a go at the previous ball, shouldered his bat and sneered at it. He was still sneering when it came in very quickly, and took the bottom of the leg stump. (Finger spin, chiefly.)

Archie walked up slowly, and gazed at me.

"Well?" I said jauntily.

"No, don't speak. I just want to look, and look, and look. It's wonderful. No elastic up the sleeve, or anything."

"This is where it first pitched," said the Major, as he examined the ground.

"Did you think of letting in a brass tablet?" I inquired shortly.

"He is quite a young man," went on Archie dreamily, "and does not care to speak about his plans for the future. But he is of opinion that— —"

"Break, break, break," said Simpson. "Three altogether."

"Look here, is there anybody else who wants to say anything? No? Then I'll go on with my over."

Archie, who had begun to walk back to his place, returned thoughtfully to me.

"I just wanted to say, old chap, that if you're writing home to-night about it, you might remember me to your people."

Blair was about the only person who didn't insult me. This was because he had been fielding long-on; and as soon as the wicket fell he moved round about fifty yards to talk to Miss Fortescue. What people can see in her— — Well, directly my next ball was bowled he started running as hard as he could to square leg, and brought off one of the finest catches I've ever seen.

"The old square-leg trap," said Archie. "But you cut it rather fine, didn't you? I suppose you knew he was a sprinter?"

"I didn't cut it at all—I was bowling. Go away."

Yes, I confess it. I did the hat trick. It was a good length half-volley, and the batsman, who had watched my first three balls, was palpably nervous. Archie walked round and round me in silence for some time, and then went over to Thomas.

"He's playing tennis with me this evening," he began.

"I was beaten at billiards by him last night," said Thomas proudly.

"He's going to let me call him by his Christian name."

"They say he's an awfully good chap when you know him," replied Thomas.

I got another wicket with the last ball of the over, and then we had lunch. Myra was smiling all over her face when we came in, but beyond a "Well bowled, Walter" (which I believe to be Brearley's name), would have nothing to do with me. Instead she seized Archie, and talked long and eagerly to him. And they both laughed a good deal.

"Arkwright," I heard Archie say at the end. "He's sure to be there, and would do it like a shot."

Like a wise captain Archie did not put me on after lunch, and Simpson soon began to have the tail in difficulties. Just after the eighth wicket fell a telegram came out. Archie took it and handed it to me. "From Maclaren, I expect," he said with a grin.

"You funny ass; I happen to know it's from Dick. I asked him for a wire about the Kent match."

"Oh, did Kent win?" said Archie, looking over my shoulder. As I opened it, the others came up, and I read—

"Please be in attendance for next Test Match."
"HAWKE"

I got three more that afternoon. One from Fry, one from Leveson-Gower, and one from Maclaren. They all came from Lord's, and I've half a mind to take my telegrams with me, and go. Then Myra would probably get six months in the second division.

"But I shouldn't mind that," said Myra. "You could easily bowl—I mean bail—me out."

A silly joke, I call it.

CHAPTER V
AT PLAY

I selected a handkerchief, gave a last look at the weather, which was beastly, and went down (very late) to breakfast. As I opened the door there was a sudden hush. Everybody looked eagerly at me. Then Miss Fortescue tittered.

Well, you know how one feels when that happens. I put my hand quickly to my tie—it was still there. I squinted down my nose, but there was no smut. To make quite sure I went over to the glass. Then Simpson exploded.

Yet nobody spoke. They all sat there watching me, and at last I began to get nervous. I opened my mouth to say "Good-morning," but before I got it out Miss Blair gave a little shriek of excitement. That upset me altogether. I walked up to the tea-pot, and pouring myself out a cup said, with exaggerated carelessness, "Rotten day, isn't it?"

And then came the laughter—shout after shout.

I held out my hand to Myra. "Good-bye," I said, "I'm going home. Thank you for a very jolly time, but I'm not going to be bullied."

"Oh, you dear," she gurgled.

"I am rather sweet before breakfast," I admitted, "but how——"

"It was too heavenly of you. I never thought you would."

"I think I shall go back to bed."

"It was rather rough luck," said Archie, "but of course the later you are the worse it is for you."

"And the higher the fewer. Quite so. If this is from Breakfast Table Topics in *The Daily Mirror*, I haven't seen them to-day; but I'll do my best."

"Archie, explain."

Archie took up a piece of paper from the table, and explained. "It's like this," he said. "I came down first and looked at the weather, and said——"

"Anyone would," I put in quickly.

"Well, then, Blair came in and said, 'Beastly day,' and then Simpson—— Well, I thought I'd write down everybody's first remark, to see if anybody let the weather alone. Here they are."

"It's awful," put in Myra, "to have one's remarks taken down straight off. I've quite forgotten what I said."

This was the list:

Archie: "Bother." (So he says.)

Blair: "What a beastly day!"

Simpson: "What a jolly day!"

The Major: "Well, not much cricket to-day, hey?"

Myra: "Oh dear, what a day!"

Miss Blair: "What a terrible day!"

Miss Fortescue: "Oh, you poor men—what a day!"

Thomas: "Rotten day, isn't it?"

Me: "Rotten day, isn't it?"

"I don't think much of Thomas's remark," I said.

Later on in the morning we met (all except the Major, that is) in the room which Myra calls hers and Archie calls the nursery, and tried to think of something to do.

"I'm not going to play bridge all day for anyone," said Archie.

"The host should lay himself out to amuse his guests," said Myra.

"Otherwise, his guests will lay him out," I warned him, "to amuse themselves."

"Well, what do you all want to do?"

"I should like to look at a photograph album," said Thomas.

"Stump cricket."

"What about hide-and-seek?"

"No, I've got it," cried Archie; "we'll be boy scouts."

"Hooray!" cried everybody else.

Archie was already on his hands and knees. "Ha!" he said, "is that the spoor of the white ant that I see before me? Spoorly not. I have but been winded by the water-beetle.

"Sound, sound the trumpet, beat the drum,
   To all the scouting world proclaim
One crowded stalk upon the turn
   Is worth an age without a name."

"Archie!" shrieked Myra in horror. "It is too late," she added, "all the ladies have swooned."

We arranged sides. Myra and I and Simpson and Thomas against the others. They were to start first.

"This isn't simply hide-and-seek," said Archie, as they went off. "You've got to track us fairly. We shall probably 'blaze' door-posts. When you hear the bleat of a tinned sardine that means we're ready. Keep your eyes skinned, my hearties, and heaven defend the right."

"We ought to have bare knees really," said Myra, when they'd gone. "Boy scouts always do. So that when they go through a bed of nettles they know they've been."

"I shall stalk the stairs to begin with," I said. "Simpson, you go down the back way and look as much like a vacuum-cleaner as possible. Then they won't notice you. Thomas and Myra— — Hush! Listen! Was that the bleat of a fresh sardine or the tinned variety?"

"Tinned," said Myra. "Let's go."

We went. I took the Queen Anne staircase on my—in the proper stalking position. I moved very slowly, searching for spoor. Half-way down the stairs my back fin slipped and I shot over the old oak at a tremendous pace, landing in the hall like a Channel swimmer. Looking up, I saw Thomas in front of me. He was examining the door for "blazes." Myra was next to him, her ear to the ground, listening for the gallop of horses' hoofs. I got up and went over to them.

"Hast seen aught of a comely wench in parlous case, hight Mistress Dahlia?" I asked Thomas.

"Boy scouts don't talk like that," he said gruffly.

"I beg your pardon. I was thinking that I was a Cavalier and you were a Roundhead. Now I perceive that you are just an ordinary fathead."

"Why," said Myra at the foot of the stairs, "what does this button mean? Have I found a clue?"

I examined it, and then I looked at my own coat.

"You have," I said. "Somebody has been down those stairs quite recently, for the button is still warm."

"Where is Scout Simpson?"

At that moment he appeared breathless with excitement.

"I have had an adventure," he said hurriedly, without saluting. "I was on the back stairs looking like a vacuum-cleaner when suddenly Archie and Miss Blair appeared. They looked right at me, but didn't seem to penetrate my disguise. Archie, in fact, leant against me, and said to Miss Blair: 'I will now tell you of my secret mission. I carry caviare—I mean despatches—to the general. Breathe but a word of this to the enemy, and I miss the half-holiday on Saturday. Come, let us be going, but first to burn the secret code.' And—and then he struck a match on me, and burned it."

Myra gurgled and hastily looked solemn again. "Proceed, Scout Simpson," she said, "for the night approaches apace."

"Well, then they started down the stairs, and I went after them on my—scouting, you know. I made rather a noise at one corner, and Archie looked round at me, and said to Miss Blair: 'The tadpoles are out full early. See yonder where one lies basking.' And he came back, and put his foot on me and said, 'Nay, 'tis but a shadow. Let us return right hastily. Yet tarry a moment, what time I lay a false trail.' So they tarried and he wrote a note and dropped it on me. And, afterwards, I got up and here it is."

"The secret despatch," cried Myra.

"It's addressed to the Scoutmistress, and it says outside: 'Private, not to be opened till Christmas Day.'"

Myra opened it and read: "Your blessed scouts are everywhere. Let me just have five minutes with her in the nursery, there's a dear. I'd do as much for you."

But she didn't read it aloud, and I didn't see it till some time afterwards. She simply put it away, and smiled, and announced that the scouts would now adjourn to the billiard-room for pemmican and other refreshments; which they did. The engagement was announced that evening.

CHAPTER VI
IN AND OUT

"Well," said Thomas, "how are we going to celebrate the joyful event?"

We were sitting on the lawn, watching Blair and Miss Fortescue play croquet. Archie and Dahlia were not with us; they had (I suppose) private matters to discuss. Our match did not begin for another hour, happily for the lovers; happily also for the croquet-players, who had about fifty-six more hoops, posts, flags and what not to negotiate.

"It's awfully difficult to realise it," said Myra. "My own brother! Just fancy—I can hardly believe it."

"I don't think there can be any doubt," I said. "Something's happened to him, anyhow—he's promised to put me in first to-day."

"Let's have a dance to-morrow night," continued Thomas, relentlessly pursuing his original idea. "And we'll all dance with Miss Blair."

"Yes. Archie would like that."

"I remember, some years ago, when I was in Spain," said Simpson——

"This," I murmured appreciatively, "is how all the best stories begin." And I settled myself more comfortably in my chair.

"No," said Simpson, "I'm wrong there. It was in Hampstead." And he returned to his meditations.

"Tell you what," said Thomas, "you ought to write 'em an ode, Simpson."

"There's nothing that rhymes with the lady."

"There's hair," I said quite unintentionally.

"I meant with Dahlia."

"My dear man, there are heaps. Why, there's azalea."

"That's only one."

"Well, there are lots of different kinds of azalea."

"Any rhymes for Archie and Mannering?" said Simpson scornfully.

"Certainly. And Simpson. You might end with him—

'"Forgive the way the metre limps on,
It's always like that with Samuel Simpson.'

You get the idea?"

"Hush," said Myra, "Miss Fortescue has passed under a hoop."

But it is time that we got on to my innings. Archie managed to win the toss, and, as he had promised, took me in with him. It was the proudest and most nervous moment of my life.

"I've never been in first before," I said, as we walked to the wickets. "Is there any little etiquette to observe?"

"Oh, rather. Especially, if you're going to take first ball."

"Oh, there's no doubt about my taking the *first* ball."

"In that case the thing to remember is, that when the umpire calls 'play' the side refusing to play loses the match."

"Then it all rests on me? Your confidence in me must be immense. I think I shall probably consent to play."

I obtained guard and took my stand at the wicket. Most cricketers nowadays, I am told, adopt the "two-eyed stance," but for myself I still stick to the good old two-legged one. It seems to me to be less wearing. My style, I should observe, blends happily the dash of a Joseph Vine with the patience of a Kenneth Hutchings; and after a long innings I find a glass of— — I've forgotten the name of it now, but I know I find it very refreshing.

Being the hero (you will admit that—after my hat trick) of this true story, I feel I must describe my innings carefully. Though it only totalled seventeen, there was this to be said for it: it is the only innings of less than a hundred ever made by a hero.

It began with a cut to square leg, for which we ran a forced single, and followed on with a brace of ones in the direction of fine slip. After that, I stopped the bowler in the middle of his run-up, and signalled to a spectator to move away from the screen. This was a put-up job with Myra, and I rather hoped they would give me something for it, but apparently they didn't. At the end of the over, I went up and talked to Archie. In first-class cricket, the batsmen often do this, and it impresses the spectators immensely.

I said, "I bet you a shilling I'm out next over."

He said, "I won't take you."

I said, "Then I huff you," and went back to my crease.

My next scoring stroke was a two-eyed hook over point's head, and then Archie hit three fours running. I had another short conversation with him, in the course of which I recited two lines from Shakespeare and asked him a small but pointed conundrum, and afterwards I placed the ball cleverly to mid-off, the agility of the fieldsman, however, preventing any increment, unearned or otherwise. Finally, I gave my cap to the umpire, made some more ones, changed my bat, and was caught at the wicket.

"I hit it," I said, as I walked away. I said it to nobody in particular, but the umpire refused to alter his decision.

"I congratulate you," said Miss Blair, when I was sitting down again.

"I was just going to do that to you," I said.

"Oh, but you were kind enough to do that last night."

"Ah, this is extra. I've just been batting out there with your young man. Perhaps you noticed?"

"Well, I think I must have."

"Yes. Well, I wanted to tell you that I think he has quite an idea of the game, and that with more experience he would probably be good enough to play for—for Surrey. Second eleven. Yes. At hockey."

"Thank you so much. You've known him a long time, haven't you?"

"We were babes together, madam. At least, simultaneously. We actually met at school. He had blue eyes and curly hair, and fought the captain on the very first day. On the second day his hair was still curly, but he had black eyes. On the third day he got into the cricket eleven, and on the fourth he was given his footer cap. Afterwards he sang in the choir, and won the competition for graceful diving. It was not until his second term that the headmaster really began to confide in him. By the way, is this the sort of thing you want?"

"Yes," smiled Dahlia. "Something like that."

"Well, then we went to Cambridge together. He never did much work, but his algebra paper in the Little Go was so brilliant that they offered him the Senior Wranglership. He refused on the ground that it might interfere with his training for the tug of war, for which he had just obtained his blue— and — — It's a great strain making all this up. Do you mind if I stop now?"

"Of course I know that isn't all true, but he is like that, isn't he?"

"He is. He put me in first to-day."

"I know you really are fond of him."

"Lorblessyou—yes."

"That makes you my friend, too."

"Of course." I patted her hand. "That reminds me—as a friend I feel bound to warn you that there is a person about in the neighbourhood called Samuel Simpson who meditates an evil design upon you and yours. In short, a poem. In this he will liken you to the azalea, which I take to be a kind of shrubby plant."

"Yes?"

"Yes, well, all I want to say is, if he comes round with the hat afterwards, don't put anything in."

"Poor man," smiled Dahlia. "That's his living, isn't it?"

"Yes. That's why I say don't put anything in."

"I see. Oh, there—he's out. Poor Archie."

"Are you very sorry?" I said, smiling at her. "I'm just going, you know."

"Between ourselves," I said later to Myra, "that isn't at all a bad girl."

"Oh, fancy!"

"But I didn't come to talk about her. I came to talk about my seventeen."

"Yes, do let's."

"Yes. Er—you begin."

CHAPTER VII
ALL OVER

"May I have a dance?" I asked Miss Blair.

She put her head on one side and considered.

"One, two, three—the next but *five*," she said.

"Thank you. That sounds a lot; is it only one?"

"You may have two running then, if you like."

"What about two running, and one hopping, and one really gliding? Four altogether."

"We'll see," said Miss Blair gravely.

Myra, who was being very busy, came up and dragged me away.

"I want to introduce you to somebody. I say, have you seen Thomas?"

"It's no earthly good introducing me to Thomas again."

"He's so important because he thinks the dance was his idea; of course I'd meant to have it all along. There she is—her name's Dora Dalton. I think it's Dora."

"I shall call her Dora, anyhow."

I was introduced, and we had a very jolly waltz together. She danced delightfully; and when we had found a comfortable corner she began to talk.

She said, "Do you play cricket?"

I was rather surprised, but I kept quite cool, and said, "Yes."

"My brother's very fond of it. He is very good too. He was playing here yesterday against Mr Mannering's team, and made six, and then the umpire gave him out; but he wasn't out really, and he was very angry. I don't wonder, do you?"

I had a sudden horrible suspicion.

"Did you say your name was Dora—I mean his name was Dalton?"

"Yes. And just because he was angry, which anybody would be, the wicket-keeper was very rude, and told him to go home and—and bake his head."

"Not bake," I said gently, my suspicion having now become almost a certainty. "Boil."

"Go home, and boil his head," she repeated indignantly.

"And did he?"

"Did he what?"

"Er—did he understand—I mean, don't you think your brother may have misunderstood? I can't believe that a wicket-keeper would ever demean himself by using the word 'boil.' Not as you might say boil. 'Cool his head' was probably the expression—it was a very hot day, I remember. And ... ah, there's the music beginning again. Shall we go back?"

I am afraid Miss Dalton's version of the incident was not quite accurate.

What had happened was this: I had stumped the fellow, when he was nearly a mile and a half outside his crease; and when he got back to it some minutes later, and found the umpire's hand up, he was extremely indignant and dramatic about it. Quite to myself, *sotto voce* as it were, I murmured, "Oh, go home!" and I may have called attention in some way to the "bails." But as to passing any remarks about boiling heads—well, it simply never occurred to me.

I had a dance with Myra shortly after this. She had been so busy and important that I felt quite a stranger. I adapted my conversation accordingly.

"It's a very jolly floor, isn't it?" I said, as I brought her an ice.

"Oh yes!" said Myra in the same spirit.

"Have you been to many floors—I mean dances, lately?"

"Oh yes!"

"So have I. I think dances have been very late lately. I think when the floor's nice it doesn't matter about the ices. Don't you think the band is rather too elastic—I mean keeps very good time? I think so long as the time is good it doesn't matter about the floor."

"Oh, *isn't* it?" said Myra enthusiastically.

There was a pleasant pause while we both thought of something else to say.

"Have you," we began.

"I beg your pardon," we said at once.

"I was going to say," Myra went on, "have you read any nice books lately, or are you fonder of tennis?"

"I like reading nice books *about* tennis," I said. "If they *are* nice books, and are really about tennis. Er—do you live in London?"

"Yes. It is so handy for the theatres, isn't it? There is no place exactly like London, is there? I mean it's so different."

"Well, of course, up in Liverpool we do get the trams, you know, now.... I say, I'm tired of pretending I've only just met you. Let's talk properly."

At this moment we heard a voice say, "Let's try in here," and Archie and Dahlia appeared.

"Hallo! here's the happy pair," said Myra.

They came in and looked at us diffidently. I leant back and gazed at the ceiling.

"Were you just going?" said Archie.

"We were not," I said.

"Then we'll stay and talk to you."

"We were in the middle of an important conversation."

"Oh, don't mind us."

"Thank you. It's really for your benefit, so you'd better listen. Let me see, where were we? Oh yes, 'One pound of beef, ninepence; three pounds of potatoes, fourpence; one piece of emery paper for the blanc-mange, tuppence; one pound of india-rubber——'"

"'Dahlia *darling*,'" interrupted Myra, in a fair imitation of Archie's voice, "'how often have I told you that we *can't* afford india-rubber in the cake? Just a few raisins and a cherry is really all you want. You *mustn't* be so extravagant.'"

"'Dearest, I do try; and after all, love, it wasn't *I* who fell into the cocoa last night.'"

"'I didn't fall in, I simply dropped my pipe in, and it was you insisted on pouring it away afterwards. And then, look at this—*One yard, of lace*, 4s. 6d. That's for the cutlets, I suppose. For people in our circumstances paper frillings are *quite* sufficient.'"

Archie and Dahlia listened to us with open mouths. Then they looked at each other, and then at us again.

"Is there any more?" asked Archie.

"There's lots more, but we've forgotten it."

"You aren't ill or anything?"

"We are both perfectly well."

"How's Miss Dalton?"

"Dora," I said, "is also well. So is Miss Fortescue and so is Thomas. We are all well."

"I thought, perhaps — — "

"No, there you are wrong."

"I expect it's just the heat and the excitement," said Dahlia, with a smile. "It takes some people like that."

"I'm afraid you miss our little parable," said Myra.

"We do. Come on, Dahlia."

"You'll pardon me, Archibald, but Miss Blair is dancing this with me."

Archie objected strongly, but I left, him with Myra, and took Miss Blair away. We sat on the stairs and thought.

"It has been a lovely week," said Dahlia.

"It has," I agreed.

"Perhaps more lovely for me than for you."

"That's just where I don't agree with you. You know, we think it's greatly over-rated. Falling in love, I mean."

"Who's 'we'?"

"Myra and I. We've been talking it over. That's why we rather dwelt upon the sordid side of it just now. I suppose we didn't move you at all?"

"No," said Dahlia, "we're settled."

"That's exactly it," I said. "I should hate to be settled. It's so much more fun like this. Myra quite agrees with me."

Dahlia smiled to herself. "But perhaps some day," she began.

"I don't know. I never look more than a week ahead. 'It has been great fun this week, and it will probably be great fun next week.' That's my motto."

"Well, ye—es," said Miss Blair doubtfully.

PART II

CHAPTER I
ONE OF THE PLAYERS

"Do I know everybody?" I asked Myra towards the end of the dinner, looking round the table.

"I think so," said Myra. "If there's anybody you don't see in the window ask for him."

"I can see most of them. Who's that tall handsome fellow grinning at me now?"

"Me," said Archie, smiling across at us.

"Go away," said Myra. "Gentlemen shouldn't eavesdrop. This is a perfectly private conversation."

"You've got a lady on each side of you," I said heatedly, "why don't you talk to *them*? It's simply scandalous that Myra and I can't get a moment to ourselves."

"They're both busy; they won't have anything to say to me."

"Then pull a cracker with yourself. Surely you can think of something, my lad."

"He has a very jealous disposition," said Myra, "and whenever Dahlia—— Bother, he's not listening."

I looked round the table again to see if I could spy a stranger.

"There's a man over there—who's he? Where this orange is pointing."

"Oranges don't point. Waggle your knife round. Oh, him? Yes, he's a friend of Archie's—Mr Derry."

"Who is he? Does he do anything exciting?"

"He does, rather. You know those little riddles in the Christmas crackers?"

"Yes?"

"Yes. Well, he couldn't very well do those, because he's an electrical engineer."

"But why——"

"No, I didn't. I simply asked you if you knew them. And he plays the piano beautifully, and he's rather a good actor, and he never gets up till about ten. Because his room is next to mine, and you can hear everything, and I can hear him not getting up."

"That doesn't sound much like an electrical engineer. You ask him suddenly what amperes are a penny, and see if he turns pale. I expect he makes up the riddles, after all. Simpson only does the mottoes, I know. Now talk to Thomas for a bit while I drink my orange."

Five minutes elapsed, or transpired (whichever it is), before I was ready to talk again. Generally, after an orange, I want to have a bath and go straight off to bed, but this particular one had not been so all-overish as usual.

"Now then," I said, as I examined the crystallised fruit, "I'm with you in one minute."

Myra turned round and looked absently at me.

"I don't know how to begin," she said to herself.

"The beginning's easy enough," I explained, as I took a dish of green sweets under my charge, "it's the knowing when to stop."

"Can you eat those and listen to something serious?"

"I'll try.... Yes, I can eat them all right. Now, let's see if I can listen.... Yes, I can listen all right."

"Then it's this. I've been putting it off as long as I can, but you've got to be told to-night. It's—well—do you know why you're here?"

"Of course, I do. Haven't I just been showing you?"

"Well, why are you here?"

"Well, frankly, because I'm hungry, I suppose. Of course, I know that if I hadn't been I should have come in to dinner, just the same, but—— Hang it, I mean that's the root idea of a dining-room, isn't it? And I am hungry. At least I was."

"Stave it off again with an almond," said Myra, pushing them along to me. "What I really meant was why you're here in the house."

This was much more difficult. I began to consider possible reasons.

"Because you all love me," I started; "because you put the wrong address on the envelope; because the regular boot-boy's ill; because you've never heard me sing in church; because—stop me when I'm getting warm—because Miss Fortescue refused to come unless I was invited; because——"

"Stop," said Myra. "That was it. And, of course, you know I didn't mean that at all."

"What an awful lot of things you don't mean to-night. Be brave, and have it right out this time."

"All right, then, I will. One, two, three—we're going to act a play on Saturday."

She leant forward, and regarded me with apprehension.

"But why not? I'll promise to clap."

"You can't, because, you see, you're going to act too. Isn't it jolly?" said Myra breathlessly.

I gave what, if I hadn't just begun the last sweet, would have been a scornful laugh.

"Me act? Why, I've never—I don't do it—it isn't done—I don't act—not on Saturdays. How absurd!"

"Have you told him, Myra?" Dahlia called out suddenly.

"I'm telling him now. I think he's taking it all right."

"Don't talk about me as 'him'!" I said angrily. "And I'm not taking it all right. I'm not taking it at all."

"It's only such a very small part—we're all doing something, you know. And your costume's ordered and everything. But how awfully sporting of you."

After that, what could I say?

"Er—what am I?" I asked modestly.

"You're a—a small rat-catcher," said Myra cheerfully.

"I beg your pardon?"

"A rat-catcher."

"You said a small one. Does that mean that I'm of diminutive size, or that I'm in a small way of business, or that my special line is young ones?"

"It means that you haven't much to say."

"I see. And would you call it a tragic or a pathetic part?"

"It's a comic part, rather. You're Hereditary Grand Rat-Catcher to the Emperor Bong. Bong the Second. Not the first Bong, the Dinner Bong."

"Look here. I suppose you know that I've never acted in my life, and never been or seen a rat-catcher in my life. It is therefore useless for you to tell me to be perfectly natural."

"You have so little to do; it will be quite easy. Your great scene is where you approach the Emperor very nervously——"

"I shall do the nervous part all right."

"And beg him to spare the life of his mother-in-law."

"Why? I mean, who is she?"

"Miss Fortescue."

"Yes, I doubt if I can make that bit seem quite so natural. Still, I'll try."

"Hooray. How splendid!"

"A rat-catcher," I murmured to myself. "Where is the rat? The rat is on the mat. The cat is on the rat. The bat is on the cat. The——"

"Mr Derry will go through your part with you to-morrow. Some of it is funnier than that."

"The electrical engineer? What do they know about rat-catching?"

"Nothing, only——"

"Aha! Now I see who your mysterious Mr Derry is. He is going to coach us."

"He is. You've found it out at last. How bright green sweets make you."

"They have to be really bright green sweets. Poor man! What a job he'll have with us all."

"Yes," said Myra, as she prepared to leave me. "Now you know why he doesn't get up till ten."

"In the rat-catching business," I said thoughtfully, as I opened the door, "the real rush comes in the afternoon. Rat-catchers in consequence never get up till ten-thirty. Do you know," I decided, "I am quite beginning to like my little part."

CHAPTER II
ALARMS AND EXCURSIONS

I was, I confess, very late the next morning, even for a rat-catcher. Mr Derry was in the middle of his breakfast; all the others had finished. We saluted, and I settled down to work.

"There is going to be a rehearsal at eleven o'clock, I believe," said Derry. "It must be nearly that now."

"I shall be there," I said, "if I have to bring the marmalade with me. You're going to coach us?"

"Well, I believe I said I would."

"Though I have never assumed the buskin myself," I went on, "I have, of course, heard of you as an amateur actor." (*Liar.*) "And if you could tell me how to act, while I am finishing my bacon, I should be most awfully obliged."

"Haven't you really done any?"

"Only once, when I was very small. I was the heroine. I had an offer, but I had to refuse it, I said, 'Alath, dear heart, I may not, I am married already.'"

"Very right and proper," murmured Derry.

"Well, as it turned out, I had made a mistake. It was my first who had been married already. The little play was full of surprises like."

Derry coughed, and took out his pipe. "Let me see," he began, "what's your part?"

"I am—er—a rodent-collector."

"Oh yes—the Emperor's rat-catcher."

"Grand hereditary," I said stiffly. "It had been in the family for years."

"Quite so."

I was about to enlarge upon the advantages of the hereditary principle when the door opened suddenly to admit Myra and Archie.

"You don't say you're down at last!" said Myra, in surprise.

"I hardly say anything at breakfast, as a rule," I pointed out.

"What an enormous one you're having. And only last night— —"

"On the contrary, I'm eating practically nothing—a nut and one piece of parsley off the butter. The fact is, I glanced at my part before I went to bed, and there seemed such a lot of it I hardly slept at all."

"Why, you don't come on very much," said Archie. "Neither do I. I'm a conjuror. Can any gentleman here oblige me with a rabbit? ... No, sir, I said a rabbit. Oh, I beg your pardon, I thought you were coming up on to the stage.... Any gentleman— —"

"Have some jam instead. What do you mean by saying I don't come on very much?" I took the book out of my pocket, and began to turn the leaves. "Here you are, nearly every page—'Enter R.,' 'Exit R.,' 'Enter L.'—I don't know who *he* is—'Exeunt R.,'—why, the rat-catcher's always doing something. Ah, here they're more explicit—'Enter R.C.' Hallo, that's funny, because I'd just— — Oh, I see."

"One of our oldest and most experienced mimes," said Archie to Derry. "You must get him to talk to you."

"No secret of the boards is hid from him," added Myra.

"Tell us again, sir, about your early struggles," begged Archie.

"He means your early performances on the stage," explained Myra.

"There's one very jolly story about Ellen Terry and the fireproof curtain. Let me see, were you *Macbeth* then, or *Noise of Trumpets*? I always forget."

I drank my last cup of tea, and rose with dignity.

"It is a humorous family," I apologised to Derry. "Their grandfather was just the same. He *would* have his little joke about the first steam-engine."

Outside, in the hall, there was a large crowd of unemployed, all talking at once. I caught the words "ridiculous" and "rehearsal," and the connection between the two seemed obvious and frequent. I singled out Thomas, abstracted his pouch, and began to fill up.

"What is all this acting business?" I asked. "Some idea about a little play, what? Let's toddle off, and have a game of billiards."

"They've let me in for a bally part," said Thomas, "and you needn't think you're going to get out of it. They've got you down, all right."

"Thomas, I will be frank with you. I am no less a person than the Emperor Bong's Hereditary (it had been in the family for years) Grand Rat-catcher. The real rush, however, comes in the afternoon. My speciality is young ones."

"I'm his executioner."

"And he has a conjuror too. What a staff! Hallo, good morning, Simpson. Are you anything lofty?"

"'Oh, I am the Emperor Bong,'" said Simpson gaily; "'I am beautiful, clever and strong— —'"

"Question," said Thomas.

"'Tis my daily delight to carouse and to fight, and at moments I burst into song.'"

I looked at him in amazement.

"Well, just at present," I said, "all I want is a match.... A lucifer, Emp. A pine vesta, Maj. Thanks.... Now tell me—does anybody beside yourself burst into song during the play? Any bursting by Thomas or myself, for instance?"

"Nobody sings at all. My little poem is recitative."

"If you mean it's very bad, I agree with you," said Thomas.

"I made it up myself. It was thought that my part should be livened up a little."

"Well, why hasn't it been?"

"If you will give me two minutes, Simpson," I said, "I will liven up my own part better than that. What rhymes with rat-catcher?"

"Cat-catcher."

"Wait a bit.... Yes, that's got it.

"'Oh, I'm on the Emperor's staff
I'm a rodent-collector (don't laugh)—
My record (in braces)
Of rats and their races
Is a thousand and eight and a half.'"

"May we have that again?" said Myra, appearing suddenly.

"'Oh, I'm on— —'"

"No," said Thomas.

"'Oh, I'm on— —'"

"No," said Simpson.

"There is no real demand, I'm afraid."

"Well, I did just hear it before," said Myra. "I wish you'd make up one for me. I think we might all announce ourselves like that, and then the audience will have no difficulty in recognising us."

"They'll recognise Thomas if he comes on with an axe. They won't think he's just trotted round with the milk. But what are you, Myra?"

"The Emperor's wife's maid."

"Another member of the highly trained staff. Well, go on, Simpson."

"'Oh, I am her Majesty's maid,'" declared Simpson. "We all begin with 'Oh,' to express surprise at finding ourselves on the stage at all. 'Oh, I am her Majesty's maid, I'm a sad little flirt, I'm afraid.'"

"I'm respectable, steady and staid," corrected Myra.

"No," I said; "I have it—"

> "'Oh, I am her Majesty's maid!
> And her charms are beginning to fade,
>   I can sit in the sun
>   And look *just* twenty-one,
> While *she's* thirty-six in the shade.'"

Myra made a graceful curtsey.

"Thank you, sir. You'll have to pay me a lot more of those before the play is over."

"Will I really?"

"Well, seeing as the Grand Hereditary One is supposed to be making up to her Majesty's confidential attendant——"

Miss Fortescue came pushing up to us.

"It is too ridiculous," she complained; "none of us know our parts yet, and if we have a rehearsal now—what do you think about it?"

I looked at Myra and smiled to myself. "I'm all for a rehearsal at once," I said.

CHAPTER III
A REHEARSAL

"Now this is a very simple trick," said Archie, from the centre of the stage. "For this little trick all I want is, a hippopotamus and a couple of rubies. I take the hippopotamus in one hand—so—and cover it with the handkerchief. Then, having carefully peeled the rubies——"

Thomas put the last strip of silver paper on to his axe, and surveyed the result proudly.

"But how splendid!" said Myra, as she hurried past. "Only you want some blood." And she jumped over the footlights and disappeared.

"Good idea. Archie, where do you keep the blood?"

"Hey, presto! it's gone. And now, sir, if you will feel in your waistcoat pockets you will find the hippopotamus in the right-hand side and the red ink in the left. No? Dear, dear, the hippopotamus must have been a bad one."

"Be an artist, Thomas," I said, "and open a vein or two. Do the thing properly, Beerbohm. But soft, a winsome maid, in sooth; I will approach her. I always forget that sooth bit. But soft, a win——"

"Why don't we begin?" asked Simpson; "I can't remember my part much longer. Oh, by the way, when you come up to me and say, 'Your Majesty e'en forgets the story of the bull's-eye and the revolving bookcase——"

"Go away; I don't say anything so silly."

"Oh, of course it's Blair. Blair, when you come up to me and say——" They retired to the back of the stage to arrange a very effective piece of business.

"Any card you like, madam, so long as it is in the pack. The Queen of Hearts? Certainly. Now I take the others and tear them up—so. The card remaining will be yours. Ah, as I thought—it is the Queen of Hearts."

"Archie, you're talking too much," said Dahlia, "and none of it comes into your part really."

"I'm getting the atmosphere. Have you an old top hat on you, dear, because if so we'll make a pudding. No top hat? Then pudding is horf."

"But stay, who is this approaching? Can it be—I say, mind the footlights. When are we going to begin?"

"There!" said Thomas proudly. "Anybody would know that was blood."

"But how perfectly lovely," said Myra. "Only you want some notches."

"What for?"

"To show where you executed the other men, of course. You always get a bit off your axe when you execute anybody."

"Yes, I've noticed that too," I agreed. "Notches, Thomas, notches."

"Why don't you do something for a change? What about the trap or whatever it is you catch your bally rats with? Why don't you make that?"

"It isn't done with a trap, Thomas dear. It's partly the power of the human eye and partly kindness. I sit upon a sunny bank and sing to them."

"Which is that?"

"If we don't begin soon," began Simpson— —

"Hallo, Emperor, what's that you're saying? Quite so, I agree with you. I wonder if your High Fatness can lend me such a thing as a hard-boiled egg. Simpkins, when this rehearsal is over—that is to say, to-morrow—I'll take you on at juggling; I'm the best— —"

Deny finished his conversation with Miss Fortescue and turned to the stage.

"Now then, please, *please*," he said. "We'll just take the First Act. Scene, The Emperor's Palace. Enter Rat-catcher. You come on from the left."

I coughed and came on.

My part was not a long one, but it was a very important one. I was the connecting link between the different episodes of the play, and they wanted some connecting. Whenever anybody came on to the stage, I said (supposing I was there, and I generally was—the rat-catcher of those days corresponding to the modern plumber)—I said, "But who is this?" or "Hush, here comes somebody." In this way, the attention of the wakeful part of the audience was switched on to the new character, and continuity of action was preserved.

I coughed and came on.

"No," said Derry, "you must come on much more briskly."

"I can't. I've been bitten by a rat."

"It doesn't say so anywhere."

"Well, that's how I read the part. Hang it, I ought to know if I've been bitten or not. But I won't show it if you like; I'll come on briskly."

I went out, and came on very briskly.

"That's better," said Derry.

"'His Majesty ordered me to be here at the stroke of noon,'" I said. "'Belike he has some secret commands to lay upon me, or perchance it is nought but a plague of rats. But who is this?'"

"'Oh,'" said Myra, coming in suddenly, "'I had thought to be alone.'"

"'Nay, do not flee from me, pretty one. It is thus that— —' I say, Myra, it's no good my saying do not flee if you don't flee."

"I was just going to. You didn't give me a chance. There, now I'm fleeing."

"Oh, all right. 'It is thus that the rats flee when they see me approaching. Am I so very fearsome?'"

"'Orrid,'" said Archie to himself from the wings.

"One moment," said Derry, and he turned round to speak to somebody.

"Puffickly 'orrid," said Archie again.

"Nay, do not frown," Myra went on, "'tis only my little brother, who is like unto a codfish himself, and jealous withal."

"Ay, ay, and I thought it *was* a codfish. So that I had e'en brought the egg-sauce with me."

"Trouble not thyself for that," said Archie. "For verily the audience will supply thee with all the eggs thou wantest. I say, we *are* being funny."

"I'm not, I'm quite serious, I really did think it was a co— — 'But tell me, fair one,'" I said hurriedly, "'for what dost the Emperor want me?'"

"Yes, yes," said Derry, "I'm sorry I had to interrupt you. I think perhaps we had better begin again. Yes, from the beginning."

The rehearsal rolled on.

"I think it went splendidly," said Myra. "If only we had known our parts and come in at the right moments and been more serious over it."

"If there's any laughing to be done it will have to be done by *us*. The audience won't laugh."

"'Mr Derry having explained that the author was not in the house, the audience collected their cauliflowers and left quietly.' I think it's a rotten play."

"Well, it isn't frightfully funny," said Myra, "but we can put that in ourselves."

"It's so jolly hard to say the lines properly—they're so unnatural," complained Thomas. "'Truly thou hast created a favourable impression with the damsel'—well, I mean, it's absurd. Any ordinary person would say 'Truly thou art amongst them, old spot,' or something of that kind."

"Well, you say that, Thomas; you'll be all right,"

"We might put a few songs in," said Dahlia, "and a dance or two."

"I think you've forgotten that we've done only Act I.," remarked Archie. "His Majesty's conjuror doesn't really let himself go till Act II. Still, I'm all for a song and a dance. Simpson, come and Apache with me."

They dashed at each other fiercely.

"Oh, *we'll* make it go all right," said Myra.

CHAPTER IV
LAST MOMENTS

"Has anybody here seen Kelly?" asked Dahlia, putting her head in at the billiard-room door. "I mean Archie."

"I'm waiting here for Kate," I said. "I mean Myra."

"Oughtn't you to be dressing? It doesn't matter about me—I'm not on for a long time."

"A rat-catcher's best suit is not an elaborate one; I can put it on in about five minutes. It is now seven-thirty, we begin at eight-thirty—hence the billiard cue. More chalk."

"Oh, why aren't you nervous? How you can stand calmly there——"

"I am nervous. Look." I aimed carefully and put the red into a pocket some miles away. "There you are. Have you ever seen me do that in real life? Of course not. If my hand had been steady I should have been a foot to the right. Still more chalk."

"Well, I want Archie, and I shall cry if I don't find him. That's how I feel." She sat down and got up again.

"My dear Dahlia," I said solemnly, "now you can understand a father's feelings—I mean, now, you see what you women have brought on yourselves. Who suggested a play? The women. Who dragged me into it? The women. Who said rat-catchers always wore whiskers? The women. Who is designing me a pair of whiskers at this moment? The wom—— Simpson. Who but for whom (this is going to be a very difficult sentence) who but for whom, would be just thinking of dressing leisurely for dinner, instead of which we had a hasty snack, and have now got to put on heaven knows what? The women. Well, it serves you right."

"Don't be horrid. I want Archie." She got up for the third time and drifted out of the room.

I chalked my cue and went into a pocket without touching anything. When I say I went in I mean that the ball I was playing with went in. You do see that? Very well, then. I took it out and began to squint along my cue again, when two hands came suddenly over my eyes and a voice said; "Guess who is is."

"The Queen of Sheba," I tried.

"Right," said Myra.

I turned and looked at her.

"Golly, you do, you really do!" I said at last. "Did they always dress like that in the Bong era? Short skirts, long pigtail, bare arms—lovely!"

"'I can sit in the sun and look just twenty-one,'" sang Myra as she dropped into the sofa.

"Well, just at present you're sitting in the billiard-room and looking about fifteen.... How are you getting on with your French this term? I had a very bad report in the holidays from your governess. The extra ninepence a week seems to have been simply thrown away."

"Aren't you excited?" said Myra, looking at me with sparkling eyes.

"As for calisthenics, well, what I say is, 'My daughter is Church of England, and if you don't like it, she can come away. I'm not going to have her stuffed up with all that nonsense.'"

Myra jumped up. "Aren't you excited?" she insisted.

"Feel my tongue—I mean my pulse, it's quite normal. And why? Because I've forgotten my part, and I'm going to bed."

"It's a great responsibility our beginning the play."

"It is. Have you ever thought that, if we refused to begin, the play couldn't continue, and then the audience would be able to go home? My idea was to tackle the people as they arrive, and come to terms with them. I'm sure there's money in it."

"You aren't bothering, are you?"

"Of course, I am. I'd give a hundred pounds to be out of it. No, I wouldn't—I'd give a hundred pounds if you'd always wear that frock and do your hair like that. Will you? And you shall go on with your French, child."

Myra curtsied prettily.

"And I'll go on with my whiskers. You haven't seen me in those yet, have you?" There was a loud noise without. "Here they are, coming in."

It was not the whiskers, however, but Archie and Thomas in full costume; Archie in green and Thomas in black.

"Hallo," said Archie, "I feel just like a conjuror."

"You look just like a grasshopper," said Thomas.

"My dear friend," said Archie, patting him kindly on his shoulder, "is that you? But you oughtn't to be here, you know. You came up the hot-water pipe, I suppose? Yes, yes, but they misdirected you—the blackbeetle department is in the basement. Well, well, it will be easier going down."

"Archie, Dahlia's looking for you."

"It's all right, she found me. She was nearly in tears. She said, 'Is that my Archibald or an onion?' I said 'Fear not, fair one, 'tis but the early crocus.' Myra, don't you think they've overdone the green rather? To be quite frank, I don't see why a conjuror should be dressed in green at all."

"To distinguish him from the rat-catcher in brown, the executioner in black, and the Master of the Gold Fish in red."

"I had thought that perhaps a certain aptitude for legerdemain might so distinguish him. But I perceive that I am wrong. Hallo, why aren't you in brown then?"

"I'm coming on like this," I explained. "I was going to have changed, but now I've seen you two, I don't think I will. With my ordinary clothes, one whisker—probably the starboard one—and a little insouciance, I shall be a great success."

"What annoys me," said Thomas, "is that in the early Bong age they had no bally pockets. I've simply got nowhere to keep a handkerchief."

"Keep it behind the scenes; and then, if you blow your nose immediately before the execution, and again immediately after it, you ought to be all right."

"It isn't for that. It's in case I want to cry."

"It's all right for me," said Archie. "I've simply got to say, 'Now can anybody in the audience oblige me with a handkerchief?' and I shall get dozens."

"Then I shall probably touch you for one. Great Irvings! is this really Simpson?"

The Emperor Bong was making a splendid entry, looking (except for his spectacles) exactly like an emperor.

"Rise, rise," he said. "Stop grovelling. Oh, look here, you fellows, when I say 'On the stomach!' then you must——Oh, I beg your pardon, Miss Mannering, I didn't see you were there."

"Where are my whiskers?" I asked sternly.

"My dear old chap, I couldn't do them; there wasn't enough to go round. I made two nice little eyebrows instead—you'll find them on your dressing-table. 'Oh, I am the Emperor Bong, I am beautiful, clever and strong. I am beauti——' Do you think I ought to wear my spectacles or not?"

There was a loud shout of "No!"

"Oh, all right. But I shall probably fall over the sunset or something. Thomas, if you see me wandering into a new moon, tap me on the head with your axe. Why isn't my rat-catcher dressed?"

"He was waiting for his whiskers."

"That's perfectly absurd. You could have grown a pair in the time. Go and dress at once."

"I refuse to do anything till a quarter-past eight," I said. "If I get into my things now, all the atmosphere will have worn off by the time we begin."

"It's worn off me a long time ago," said Thomas dismally.

"And me," said Myra, with a shiver.

"Well, we're all very miserable," said Archie; "let's have a bottle of something. What? Oh, hush! Simpson, just ring the bell, and I'll show you a little conjuring trick. There's nothing on the table at present, is there? No. Well, now, you watch."

CHAPTER V
THE NIGHT

The play was a great success; I know, because many of the audience told me so afterwards. Had they but guessed what was going on behind the scenes, the congratulations would have been even more enthusiastic. For as near as a touch we had to drop the eggproof curtain and hand the money back.

I am going to give you the opening scene as it was actually said—not as it was heard across the footlights—and then you will understand. As you may remember, the *Rat-catcher* (Me) and the *Maid* (Myra) take the stage first, and they introduce themselves in the usual way to the audience and each other. The scene is the palace of the *Emperor Bong* (Simpson). Very well then.

Maid (*sweetly*). Truly his Majesty is a handsome man, and I wonder not that his people love him.

Rat-catcher (*rather nervous*). Thou surprisest me. I saw him in the wings—in the winter garden just now—that is to say, anon—and thought him plain. But hush, here he comes.

(*They salaam, or whatever you call it, and stay there.*)

Rat-catcher (*still salaaming*). What's the silly ass waiting for? I can't stick this much longer; the blood's all going to my head like anything.

Maid (*in a similar position*). He must have forgotten his cue. Can't you say, "Hush, here he comes" again?

Rat-catcher. I can't say anything out loud in this position. Do you think I might come up for a breath?

Maid (*loudly*). His Majesty tarries.

Rat-catcher (*sotto voce*). He does. You've got it.

Maid. Whatever shall we do? Do think of something.

Rat-catcher. Well, I'm going to rise to the surface. I'm tired of being a submarine. (*They both stand up.*)

Maid (*brilliantly*). Perchance it was a rat we heard and not his Majesty.

Rat-catcher (with equal brilliance). Fear not, fair damsel. Behold, I will investigate. (*Proceeds to back of stage.*)

Archie (from wings). Come off, you idiot.

Rat-catcher (always the gentleman—to Maid). Tarry a while, my heart, what time I seek assistance. (*Exit.*)

Maid (confidentially to audience—to keep the thing going). Truly he is a noble youth, though he follows a lowly profession. 'Tis not the apparel that proclaims the man. Me thinks....

Me (annoyed). Who's an idiot?

Archie. Didn't you see me wink? That ass Simpson's banged his nose against a door-post and is bleeding like a pig. Says it's because he hadn't got his spectacles.

Me (still annoyed). More likely the champagne.

Archie. They're dropping keys down his back as hard as they can. Will you and Myra gag a bit, till he's ready?

Me (excitedly). My good fool, how on earth— —

Myra (coming to back of stage). But behold he returns. (*Frowns imperiously.*)

Rat-catcher (coming on again very unwillingly). Ah, fair maid, 'tis thee. I bring thee good tidings. I met one in the ante-room, a long-legged, scurvy fellow, who did tell me that his Majesty was delayed on some business.

Maid. That must have been his Conjuror—I know him well. (*Aside.*) What's happened?

Rat-catcher. Let us then rest a while, an it please thee. (*Seizing her by the arm.*) Over here. That ass Simpson's hurt himself. We've got to amuse the audience till he's finished bleeding.

Maid (sitting down with her back to audience). I say, is it really serious?

Rat-catcher. Not for him; it is for us. Now then, talk away.

Maid. Er—h'm. (*Coyly.*) Wilt not tell me of thy early life, noble sir, how thou didst become a catcher of rats?

Rat-catcher (disgusted). You coward! (*Aloud.*) Nay, rather let me hear of thine own life. (*Aside.*) Scored.

Maid. That's not fair. I asked you first. (*Modestly.*) But I am such a little thing, and you are so noble a youth.

Rat-catcher. True. (*Having a dash at it.*) 'Twas thus. My father, when I was yet a child, didst—did—no, didst—apprentice me to a salad binger— —

Maid (*with interest*). How dost one bing salads?

Rat-catcher (*curtly*). Ballad singer. And I would frequent the market-place at noon, singing catches and glees, and receiving from the entranced populace divers coins, curses, bricks and other ornaments. One morn, as I was embarked upon a lovely ballad, "Place me amidst the young gazelles," I was seized right suddenly from behind. (*Bored to death.*) I'm sick of this. We're supposed to be amusing the audience.

Maid. Oh, go on, I'm getting awfully amused.

Emperor (*audibly from green-room*). Confound it, it's begun again.

Executioner (*bitterly*). And to think that I spent hours putting red ink on my axe!

Maid (*with great presence of mind*). What's that? Surely that was a rat.

Rat-catcher (*greatly relieved*). It was. (*Getting up.*) Let's have Archie on, and see if he can amuse them a bit more. (*Aloud.*) I must finish my tale anon. Stay here, sweet child, what time I fetch my trusty terrier. (*Exit.*)

Maid. 'Tis a strange story he tells. How different from my own simple life. Born of proud but morbid parents....

Archie. What's up? Stick to it.

Me. Have you got such a thing as a trusty terrier on you?

Archie (*feeling up his sleeve*). No.

Me. Well, the audience will be extremely disappointed if I don't bring one back. I practically promised them I would. Look here, why don't you come on and help? Everybody is getting horribly bored with us.

Archie (*delightedly*). Oh, all right.

Enter Rat-catcher *and Conjuror.*

Maid. But behold he returns *again*!

Rat-catcher (*excitedly*). Great news, fair lady, which this long-legged, scurvy fellow I told you of will impart to us.

Maid. Why, 'tis the Conjuror. Have you news for us, sir?

Conjuror (*with no illusions about the Oriental style*). Absolutely stop press. What is it you want to know? Racing? The Bong Selling Plate was won by Proboscis, McSimp up. Immense enthusiasm. Bank rate unchanged—quite right this cold weather. Excuse me a moment, sir, your moustache is coming off. No, the left wing—allow me to lend you a postage stamp. Do you prefer red or green?

Maid (biting her lip). Will you not give us news of the Emperor?

Conjuror. I will. His Majesty has met with a severe accident whilst out hunting this morning, being bitten by a buffalo.

Maid. Alas, what will my mistress say?

Conjuror. She has already said everything that was necessary. Her actual words were: "Just like Bong."

Rat-catcher (seizing the opportunity). His Majesty ordered me to meet him here at noon. Methinks I had better withdraw and return anon. *(Makes off hurriedly.)*

Conjuror (seizing him). Not so. He bade me command you to stay and sing to us. *(Sensation.)*

Rat-catcher (huskily). Alas, I have forgotten my voice—that is, I have left my music at home. I will go and fetch it. *(Has another dash.)*

Conjuror. Stay! Listen! *(They all listen.)*

Simpson (in wings). Thanks, thanks, that will be all right now. Oh no, quite, thanks. Oh, is this your key? Thanks, thanks. No, it doesn't matter about the other ones, they don't feel at all uncomfortable, thanks. Yes, I think it really did stop it, thanks.

Conjuror. I'm off! *(Aloud.)* His Majesty has regained consciousness. *(Exit.)*

Simpson (apologetically). Oh, Archie, I've got the billiard-room key in my— —

Rat-catcher (very loudly to Maid*).* Hush, here he comes! *(They salaam.)*

(Enter the Emperor Bong.)

CHAPTER VI
THE CURTAIN GOES DOWN

"Ladies and gentlemen," said Simpson at the supper-table, glass in hand, "it is my pleasant duty——"

"Bother!" murmured Myra. "Drinking healths always makes me feel funny."

"Silence for McSimp," shouted Archie. "Now then, pass along there, please. There's no need to push, you'll all be able to hear. Gentlemen, the O'Sumph is addressing us impromptu, not to say unasked."

"It is my pleasant duty," continued Simpson, "as your late Emperor (*Half-an-hour-late. How's the probosc?*), to propose the health of the Rabbits Dramatic Company. (*Hooray!*) Great as we are on the cricket-field (*Wide!*)— great, I say, as we are on the cricket-field (*Pitch 'em up, Simpson*), we are, I think, still greater in the halls of Thespis. (*Don't know the lady.*) Gentlemen, I knew Irving. (*Liar!*) I have heard tell of Garrick (*Good! Ever heard of Shakespeare?*), but to-night has been a new experience for me. (*I will—give you—the kee—eys of——.*) Ladies and gentlemen, I propose our very good healths, coupled with the name of our hostess Miss Mannering." (*Loud Cheers.*)

"That's me," said Myra.

"I single out Miss Mannering," added Simpson, "because I'm sure we should all like to hear her make a speech."

"Oh, Samuel," said Myra, shaking her head at him, "and I thought it was because you loved me."

"The Rabbits! Myra!" we cried.

"Miss Mannering will now address you," announced Archie. "She will be glad to answer any questions afterwards; but anyone who interrupts will be hurled out. I appeal to you, as Englishmen, to give her a fair hearing."

Myra stood on a chair, looking lovely, but very lonely, and waited till we were silent.

"My dear good friends," she began, and then she caught Thomas's eye. "Hallo, Tommy," she said wistfully.... "My dear good friends, but why should you say *I'm* a jolly good fellow, when it isn't my birthday or anything? But how *silly* of you! Why, of course, we're *all* jolly good fellows—and jolly good actors too. It *has* been fun, hasn't it? ... Oh, Archie, dear.... I hope we shall all be here in the summer, don't you? Well, you can't very well say you don't, now I've asked you, can you? You'll have to pretend your uncles are very ill, and then you needn't come.... Oh, *please—don't* look at me like that, you make me want to cry, and I only want to laugh to-night.... Archie, may I get down?"

"She *is* a dear," Dahlia whispered to me. "How you can go on——"

It was Simpson who saved the situation and made us merry and bright again. He hastily trotted out the suggestion that we should tour the country in the summer, playing cricket in the day and *Bong the Second* at night. Archie backed him up at once.

"Only I'm off Bong Two altogether," he said. "Of course, what we want is a cricket play. We shall have to write one ourselves, I expect; there aren't any really good ones about. Act I. Rupert Vavasour, a dashing bat and the last descendant of an ancient but impoverished house, is in love with the beautiful but equally impoverished Millicent. Milly is being pursued by a rich villain of the name of Jasper Fordyce, the said Jasper being a bowler of extreme swiftness, with a qualification for Essex.... Go on, Simpson."

"In order to restore the fallen fortunes of the house, Rupert plays for Kent as a professional—Binks (R.)—and secures talent money in six successive matches. Jasper hears of it, and (Act II.) assassinates the scorer, bribing a hireling of his own to take the deceased's place. In the next match Rupert only scores forty-nine."

"Rupert," continued Thomas, "who had been counting his own jolly score, and made it eighty-seven, was furious, and determined at all costs to foil the villain. Accordingly he went on to bowl in the next innings and took five wickets for two hundred and thirty-nine, thus obtaining talent money."

"A little love interest, please, Dahlia," said Archie.

"Now the captain, who was in the secret," said Dahlia, "was in love with Rupert's sister, which was why he put Binks (R.) on to bowl. As soon as Binks had collected his five wickets, Blythe went on, and took the other five for three runs. In this way Kent just managed to win, and so Rupert got more talent money."

"The next match was against Essex—Act III., the great act of the play— and Jasper Fordyce was playing for the Leyton brigade. As he put on his spurs before taking the field, and brushed his sleek black hair, he smiled sardonically to himself. Had he not overnight dug holes in the pitch at the pavilion end, and was not the wicket fiery, and he notoriously an erratic bowler?"

"Everything points to Simpson playing Jasper," I said, and continued:

"'Heads,' cried Jasper. It was heads. 'I put you in,' he remarked calmly. 'What!' said the other in amazement. Ten minutes later Binks (R.) and Humphreys were at the wicket. Binks took first ball with a touch of nervousness at his heart. All depended on this match. If only he could make four hundred and fifty to-day, he would be able to pay off the mortgage and marry his Millicent.... 'Play.' Jasper rushed up to the wicket and delivered the ball. Then before anybody could see how it happened, Rupert was stretched full-length upon the sward!"

"I had rather thought of playing Rupert myself," said Archie. "But I'm not so sure now."

"Five for two hundred and thirty-nine," I reminded him. "The part was written for you."

"But what of Millicent?" said Myra. "Fearing lest some evil should overtake her lover she had attended the match clad in a long ulster, and now she flung this off, revealing the fact that she was in flannels. With her hair tucked up beneath her county cap she looked a slim and handsome boy. To rush on to the field and take the injured one's place was the work of a moment. 'Who is this?' said the umpires in amazement. 'Fear not,' whispered Millicent to Humphreys, 'I have a birth qualification for the county, and the gardener coached me for an hour last night.'"

"Once more Jasper rushed up to the crease, and the spectators held their breath."

"I'm going to be a spectator," I said, "with a breath-holding part. Sorry—go on, Blair."

"Then Millicent's bat flashed, and, behold! the ball was on the boundary! A torrent of cheers rent the air. Again he bowled, again the bat flashed. Jasper ground his teeth."

"The curtain goes down here to represent the passing of an hour. When it rises again, Millicent's score is four hundred and twenty-three. There was dead silence for a moment. Then Millicent swung her bat. And at that the cheers broke out, such cheering as had never been heard before. Maclaren's record score was beaten at last! 'Now surely he will knock his wickets down,' said the spectators. Little did they know that until four hundred and fifty was upon the tins the mortgage could not be paid off! Four hundred and thirty—four hundred and forty—four hundred and forty-nine—a sharply run single—four hundred and fifty! From the pavilion Rupert heard the cheers and fainted again."

"It was 'over,' and Millicent had the bowling. Jasper delivered the ball, a fast half-volley— —"

("Oh, Simpson simply *must* play Jasper.")

" —and Millicent drove it back hard and true. Jasper tried to duck, but it was too late. He was dead."

"Act IV. All his money went to Rupert, who was a distant cousin. He married Millicent, and they lived happily ever after. But, though they are always to be seen at the Tonbridge and Canterbury weeks, they have never played cricket again. *Curtain.*"

"And bedtime," said Myra suddenly. "Good-night, everybody."

MARGERY

TO MARGERY—FROM HER UNCLE

My dear Margery,—When I heard that you really had arrived, I got out the broken tea-cup, filled it at the bath, and drank "To my niece!" with the greatest enthusiasm possible. Had I been on the stage I should then have hurled the cup over my shoulder; and later on the scene-shifter would have come and collected the bits. As it was, I left that part out; and you will forgive me, will you not, dear baby, when you hear that it was your uncle's last cup, and he in a bad way financially.

Personally I was all for coming to see you at once. But you wrote that you would prefer me to postpone my visit for a week; at the end of which time you would have settled down, and I should be more in a position to do you justice—the critic, rather than the mere reporter. I don't know if those were quite your words, but that at any rate was the idea. So, baby, here I am—a week later, and just returned from seeing you. What, you wish to know, were my impressions?

It is like your cool way, asking me what I think of you. It was you who were to have been interviewed by *me*. You were a stranger, one short week on our shores; and I wanted to ask you what you thought of the English ladies, what were your views on our climate and (above all) what was your opinion of the English press. My editor had heard of your landing, and those were the things he wished to know. Well, I shall say that your views were undecided. Two kicks, a cry, and something very like a sneeze—you haven't quite got the hang of our language yet.

You know, Margery, there was at one time some talk of your being a boy; and, in that case, your father and I had decided that you were to play for Kent. I was to have bowled to you every evening, and he would have stood by and said, "You should have come forward to that one, sir." At the public schools they call this "coaching." However, that dream is over now, and the most we can hope for is that you should marry someone in the eleven. Your father and I were discussing it last night (in front of you—oh, what would Mrs Grundy say?), and we had almost fixed on Woolley; but your mother objected because he was a professional. A trivial reason, dear Margery, but you know what women are. You gave a little cry just at that moment, and I know you meant, "Well, why not Mr Hutchings then?" Well, we had thought of him, only your mother says he will be too old. I do hope, baby, that when you grow up you will be guided by what your heart says, and not by what your mother says....

Your mother—I think you must be careful in your dealings with that woman. Above all, do not let her prejudice you against your uncle. At one time yesterday we were discussing your personal features. "Her grannie's mouth," said somebody; "her father's nose," volunteered another. "Look at the darling's eyes, just like her loving mummy's," was that shameless person's own contribution. Then I in haste, "But, I say, what about her uncle?"

Margery, your mother looked at you thoughtfully. She looked at you every way. And then suddenly, in triumph, she cried, "Why, nurse! Of course! Her uncle's hair!"

They tell me, Margery, that as a matter of fact your name is Marjorie; and they say that the other reminds them too much of Margarine. That just shows how ignorant they are. I looked up "margarine," in the dictionary, and it is called so because of its "pearly lustre." If that isn't good enough for them, they must be a very proud couple. Anyhow, you are Margery to me: I hope I have a mind above your commonplace Marjories.

There are many things that I have to say to you, but I feel quite sure that your mother reads your letters; so perhaps I had better wait till I can see you alone. I want you always to insist on wearing shoes, as a little girl, and not those ghastly thirty-nine-button boots; also on going to one of the very big schools if you go to a boarding school at all. And I want—but I must talk to your father about it. I like to think he is still my ally. Time was when he too knew all about the bringing up of children, and though he has handicapped himself by marrying, yet now and then, when we are alone together, he is almost sensible on the subject.

Good-bye. Give my love to your mother. Perhaps we can trust her more than we thought, after all. Ever your loving UNCLE

TO HER UNCLE—FROM MARGERY

My dear Uncle,—Thank you for your letter. I was just as glad when they told me about *you*! And I said to myself, "I must be very nice to him, because mother and I have been here for years and years simply, and he's quite new." And it's unkind of you to say I kicked, I was only stretching, and one must stretch or one will never grow. I heard nurse tell mother that, and you *know* you'd like to have a tall niece.

I think I shall like you, if you're sure you won't mind my being only a girl. I don't think father minds, although he looks very sad about something every now and then. He came back late from the office the other day, and mother told me he'd done such a lot of work, and was so tired, and I cried all night about it, I was so sorry for him.

Mother *is* a funny person. This morning I did my trick of opening one eye and keeping the other shut, and she got fearfully excited, and called out "Nurse, nurse, what's the matter with baby, she can't open one of her eyes!" And then I simply *had* to open it, so as I could wink at nurse to show her what a silly mother we had. But I have given up my other joke, of pretending to be dead. I used to do it every night, and she would creep out of bed, and come and listen at my cradle, and.... Well, I'm only a girl, and I shall never go to a public school, but still I know when a joke ceases to be a joke and becomes bad form. So I have given it up.

Oh, talking of bad form, some chemists who had read about me in the papers sent me a sample of *tooth* powder. In rather doubtful taste, I thought....

I want you to come and see me have my bath. Mother asks all her friends, so why shouldn't I ask mine? Of course, I would rather keep it private, but if mother is going to make a show of it we may as well have the right people there. Do you know, uncle, they actually do it in a *basin*, although there's a proper bath just next door! I know I'm small, but is it quite fair always to be harping on the fact? (Twice a day, if you will believe me.) Of course, mother and nurse are only women, and they wouldn't understand this. But I am sure you, uncle, would be more careful of people's feelings.

I am sorry, dear, but I don't think I shall be able to marry either Mr Hutchings or Mr Woolley; you see they *are* rather old for me, *aren't* they? Mother told me yesterday that there is a dear little boy of four or five playing about somewhere, who will come for me one day and take me right away from her and father. *Fancy!* What fun!

About my name. Well, I'm afraid it will have to be *Marjorie* after all. Of course, I should prefer it to be *Margery*, but mother assures me that the owner of the name is *never* consulted, so I can't say anything. But I will always be Margery to you, and we won't say anything more about it to the others. Do you see, dear?

And now I must say good-bye, as mother says I want to go to sleep. She is writing this for me, and some of the things she didn't want to say at all, but I threatened her with my joke, and then she did. But we both send our love. Your affectionate niece, MARGERY

P.S. 1.—I was weighed yesterday. I weigh quite a lot of pounds.

P.S. 2.—Come to-morrow at four, and I will show you my toes.

MARGERY'S SOCK

CHAPTER I

When Margery was three months old I wrote a letter to her mother:

"DEAR MADAM,—If you have a copy in Class D at 1s. 10d. net, I shall be glad to hear from you. I am, THE BABY'S UNCLE"

On Tuesday I got an answer by the morning post:

"DEAR SIR,—In reply to yours: How dare you insult my child? She is in Class A1, priceless, and bought in by the owner. Four months old and two days on Christmas Day. Fancy! I am,

"THE BABY'S MOTHER"

Margery had been getting into an expensive way of celebrating her birthday every week. Hitherto I had ignored it. But now I wrote:

"DEAR MADAM,—Automatically your baby should be in Class D by now. I cannot understand why it is not so. Perhaps I shall hear from you later on with regard to this. Meanwhile I think that the extraordinary coincidence (all but two days) of the baby's birthday with Christmas Day calls for some recognition on my part. What would Margery like? You, who are in constant communication with her, should be able to tell me. I hear coral necklaces well spoken of. What do you think? I remember reading once of a robber who 'killed a little baby for the coral on its neck'—which shows at any rate that they are worn. Do you know how coral reefs are made? It is a most fascinating business.

"Then there is a silver mug to be considered. The only thing you can drink out of a mug is beer; yet it is a popular present. Perhaps you, with your (supposed) greater knowledge of babies, will explain this. Meanwhile I am,

"THE BABY'S UNCLE"

"P.S.—Which is a much finer thing than a mother."

To which her mother:

"MY DEAR BOY,—It is too sweet of you to say you would like to get baby something. No, I don't know how coral reefs are made, and I don't want to. I think it is wicked of you to talk like that; I'm sure I sha'n't dare to let her wear anything valuable now. And I don't think she really wants a mug.

"I'm sure I don't know what she does want, except to see her uncle (There!), but it ought to be something that she'll value when she grows up. And of course we could keep it for her in the meantime.

"Her father has smoked his last cigar to-day. Isn't it awful? I have forbidden him to waste his money on any more, but he says he *must* give me five hundred for a Christmas present. If he does, I shall give him that sideboard that I want so badly, and then we shall both go to prison together. You will look after baby, won't you? I am,

"THE BABY'S MOTHER"

"*P.S.*—Which she isn't proud, but does think it's a little bit classier than an uncle."

And so, finally, I;

"DEAR CHILD,—I've thought of the very thing. I am, THE BABY'S UNCLE"

That ends Chapter I. Here we go on to

CHAPTER II

Chapter II finds me in the toy department of the Stores.

"I want," I said, "a present for a child."

"Yes, sir. About how old?"

"It must be quite new," I said sternly. "Don't be silly. Oh, I see. Well, the child is only a baby."

"Ah, yes. Now here—if it's at all fond of animals——"

"I say, you mustn't call it 'IT.' *I* get in an awful row if *I* do. Of course, I suppose it's all right for you, only—well, be careful, won't you?"

The attendant promised, and asked whether the child was a boy or a girl.

"And had you thought of anything for the little girl?"

"Well, yes. I had rather thought of a sideboard."

"I beg your pardon?"

"A sideboard."

"The Sideboard Department is upstairs. Was there anything else for the little girl?"

"Well, a box of cigars. Rather full, and if you have any——"

"The Cigar Department is on the ground floor."

"But your Lord Chamberlain told me I was to come here if I wanted a present for a child."

"If you require anything in the toy line——"

"Yes, but what good are toys to a baby of four months? Do be reasonable."

"What was it *you* suggested? A sideboard and a cigar?"

"That was my idea. It may not be the best possible, but at least it is better than perfectly useless toys. You can always blow smoke in its face, or bump its head against the sideboard. *Experto crede*, if you have the Latin."

Whereupon with great dignity I made my way to the lift.

In the Sideboard Department I said: "I want a sideboard for a little girl of four months, and please don't call her 'IT.' I nearly had a row with one of your downstairs staff about that."

"I will try to be careful, sir," he replied. "What sort of a one?"

"Blue eyes, and not much hair, and really rather a sweet smile.... Was that what you wanted to know?"

"Thank you, sir. But I meant what sort of a sideboard?"

I took him confidentially by the arm.

"Look here," I said, "you know how, when one is carrying a baby about, one bumps its head on all the corners? Well, not too much of that. The mothers don't really like it, you know. They smile at the time, but ... Well, not too many corners.... Yes, I like that very much. No, I won't take it with me."

The attendant wrote out the bill.

"Number, sir?"

"She's the first. That's why I'm so nervous. I've never bought a sideboard for a child before."

"Your Stores number, I mean, sir."

"I haven't got one. Is it necessary?"

"Must have a number, sir."

"Then I'll think of a nice one for you.... Let's see—12345, now does that strike you?"

"And the name?"

"Oh, I can't tell you that. You must look that up for yourself. Good-day."

Downstairs I bought some cigars.

"For a little girl of four months," I said, "and she likes them rather full. Please don't argue with me. All your men chatter so."

"I must," said the attendant. "It's like this. If she is only four months, she is obviously little. Your observation is therefore tautological."

"As a matter of fact," I said hotly, "she is rather big for four months."

"Then it was a lie."

"Look here, you give me those cigars, and don't talk so much. I've already had words with your Master of the Sideboards and your Under-Secretary for the Toy Department.... Thank you. If you would kindly send them."

CHAPTER III

So there it is. I have given the spirit, rather than the actual letter, of what happened at the Stores. But that the things have been ordered there is no doubt. And when Margery wakes up on Christmas Day to find a sideboard and a box of cigars in her sock I hope she will remember that she has chiefly her mother to thank for it.

HOW TO PLAY THE PIANOLA

(FOREWORD.—Margery wishes me to publish the following correspondence, which has recently passed between us. It occurs to me that the name under which I appear in it may perhaps need explanation. I hate explanations, but here it is.

When Margery was eight months old she was taught to call me "Uncle." I must suppose that at this time I was always giving her things—things she really wanted, such as bootlaces, the best china, evening papers, and so on—which had been withheld by those in authority. Later on these persons came round to my way of thinking, and gave her—if not the best china, at any rate cake and bread-and-butter. Naturally, their offerings, being appreciated at last, were greeted with the familiar cry of "Uncle." "No, dear, not 'Uncle,'—'Thank-you'" came the correction.)

I

DEAR THANKYOU,—I've some wonderful news for you! Guess what it is, but no, you never will. Well, I'll tell you. *I can walk!* Really and really.

It is most awfully interesting. You put one foot out to the right, and then you bring the left after it. That's one walk, and I have done seven altogether. You have to keep your hands out in front of you, so as to balance properly. That's all the rules—the rest is just knack. I got it quite suddenly yesterday. It is such fun; I wake up about five every morning now, thinking of it.

Of course, I fall down now and then. You see, I'm only beginning. When I fall, mother comes and picks me up. That reminds me. I don't want you to call me "baby" any more, now I can walk. Babies can't walk, they just get carried about and put in perambulators. I was given a lot of names a long time ago, but I forget what they were. I think one was something rather silly, like Margery, but I have never had it used lately. Mother always calls me O.D. now.

Good-bye. Write directly you get this. Your loving O.D.

II

MY DEAR O.D.,—I was so glad to get your letter, because I was just going to write to you. What do you think? No, you'll never guess—shall I tell you?—no—yes—no; well, I've bought a pianola!

It's really rather difficult to play it properly. I know people like Paderewski and—I can only think of Paderewski for the moment—I know that sort of person doesn't think much of the pianola artist; but they are quite wrong about it all. The mechanical agility with the fingers is nothing, the soul is everything. Now you can get the soul, the *con molto expressione* feeling, just as well in the pianola as in the piano. Of course you have to keep a sharp eye on the music. Some people roll it off just like a barrel-organ; but when I see *Allegro* or *Andante* or anything of that kind on the score, I'm on it like a bird.

No time for more now, as I've just got a new lot of music in. Your loving THANKYOU

P.S.—When are you coming to hear me play? I did "Mumbling Mose" just now, with one hand and lots of soul. (Signed) PADEREWSKI

P.P.S.—I am glad you can walk.

III

DEAR THANKYOU,—I am rather upset about my walking. You remember I told you I had done seven in my last? Well, this morning I couldn't do a single one! Well, I did do one, as a matter of fact, but I suppose some people would say it didn't count, because I fell down directly after, though I don't see that that matters—do you, Thankyou? But even with that one it was only one, and yet I know I did seven the day before. I wonder why it is. I do it the right way, I'm sure, and I keep my hands out so as to balance, so perhaps it's the shoes that are wrong. I must ask mother to get me a new pair, and tell the man they're for walks.

Now *do* write me a nice long letter, Thankyou, because I feel very miserable about this. It *is* right, isn't it, when you have the right leg out, only to bring the left one just up to it, and not beyond? And does it matter which foot you start with? Let me know quickly, because father is coming home to-morrow and I want to show him. Your loving

O.D.

P.S.—I am glad you like your pianola.

IV

DEAR O.D.,—Very glad to get yours. If you really want a long letter, you shall have one; only I warn you that, if once I begin, nothing less than an earthquake can stop me. Well, first then, I played the "Merry Widow Waltz" yesterday to Mrs Polacca, who is a great authority on music, and in with all the Queen's Hall set, and she said that my touch reminded her of—I've forgotten the man's name now, which is rather sickening, because it spoils the story a bit, but he was one of the real tip-toppers who make hundreds a week, and, well—that was the sort of man I reminded her of. If I can do that with a waltz, it stands to reason that with something classic there'd be no holding me. I think I shall give a recital. Tickets 10s. 6d. No free seats. No emergency exit. It is a great mistake to have an emergency exit at a recital....

(Three pages omitted.)

Really, O.D., you must hear me doing the double F in the "Boston Cake Walk" to get me at my best. You've heard Kubelik on the violin? Well, it's not a bit like that, and yet there's just that something which links great artists together, no matter what their medium of expression. Your loving

THANKYOU

P.S.—Glad you're getting on so well with your walking.

V

DEAREST THANKYOU,—Hooray, hooray, hooray—I did twenty-five walks to-day! Father counted. He says my style reminds him of *Cancer Vulgaris* rather. How many times can *he* do it? Not twenty-five on the third day, I'm sure.

Isn't it splendid of me? I see now where I was wrong yesterday. I got the knack again suddenly this morning, and I'm all right now. To-morrow, I shall walk round the table. It is a longish way, and there are four turns, which I am not sure about. How *do* you turn? I suppose you put the right hand out? Your very loving O.D.

VI

DEAR O.D.,—I am rather hurt by your letters. I have written several times to tell you all about my new pianola, and you don't seem to take any interest at all. I was going to have told you this time that the man in the flat below has sent me a note, just as if it had been a real piano. He says he doesn't mind my playing all day, so long as I don't start before eight in the morning, as he is in his bath then, and in listening to the music quite forgets to come out sometimes, which, I can see, might be very awkward. Write to yours affectionately, THANKYOU

VII

DARLING THANKYOU,—I am so sorry, dear, and I will come and hear your pianola to-morrow, and I think it lovely, and you must be clever to play so well; but you mustn't be angry with me because I am so taken up with my walking. You see, it is all so new to me. I feel as though I want everybody to know all about it.

Your pianola must be lovely, Thankyou. *Dear* Thankyou, could you, do you think, put all the letters we wrote to each other about my walking in some book, so that other people would know how to do it the way I do? You might call it "Letters on Walking," or "How to Walk," or—but you could get a better title than I could. *Do!* Your very loving O.D.

P.S.—I'm so glad about the pianola, and do you mind if I just tell you that I *did* walk round the table, corners and all?

VIII

DEAREST O.D.,—Right you are. I will think of a good title. Your loving THANKYOU

THE KNIGHT OF THE CHIMNEY-PIECE

We don't know his real name, but we have decided to call him Arthur. ("Sir Arthur," I suppose he would be.) He stands in bronze upon the chimney-piece, and in his right hand is a javelin; this makes him a very dangerous person. Opposite him, but behind the clock (Coward!), stands the other fellow, similarly armed. Most people imagine that the two are fighting for the hand of the lady on the clock, and they aver that they can hear her heart beating with the excitement of it; but, to let you into the secret, the other fellow doesn't come into the story at all. Only Margery and I know the true story. I think I told it to her one night when she wouldn't go to sleep—or perhaps she told it to me.

The best of this tale (I say it as the possible author) is that it is modern. It were easy to have invented something more in keeping with the knight's armour, but we had to remember that this was the twentieth century, and that here in this twentieth century was Sir Arthur on the chimney-piece, with his javelin drawn back. For whom is he waiting?

"It all began," I said, "a year ago, when Sir Arthur became a member of the South African Chartered Incorporated Co-operative Stores Society Limited, Ten per cents at Par (Men only). He wasn't exactly a real member, having been elected under Rule Two for meritorious performances, Rule One being that this club shall be called what I said just now; but for nearly a year he enjoyed all the privileges of membership, including those of paying a large entrance fee and a still larger subscription. At the end of a year, however, a dreadful thing happened. They made a Third Rule—to wit, that no member should go to sleep on the billiard-table.

"Of course, Sir Arthur, having only got in under Rule Two, had to resign. He had already paid his large entrance fee, and (as it happened) his second year's subscription in advance. Naturally, he was annoyed....

"And that, in fact, is why he stands on the chimney-piece with his javelin drawn back. He is waiting for the secretary. Sir Arthur is considered to be a good shot, and the secretary wants all the flowers to be white."

At this point, Margery said her best word, "Gorky," which means "A thousand thanks for the verisimilitude of your charming and interesting story, but is not the love element a trifle weak?" (Margery is a true woman.)

"We must leave *something* to the imagination," I pleaded. "The secretary no doubt had a delightful niece, and Sir Arthur's hopeless passion for her, after he had hit her uncle in a vital spot, would be the basis of a most powerful situation."

Margery said "Gorky," again, which, as I have explained, means, "Are such distressing situations within the province of the Highest Art?"

When Margery says "Gorky" twice in one night it is useless to argue. I gave in at once. "Butter," I said, "placed upon the haft of the javelin would make it slip, and put him off his shot. He would miss the secretary and marry the niece." So we put a good deal of butter on Sir Arthur, and for the moment the secretary is safe. I don't know if we shall be able to keep it there; but in case jam does as well, Margery has promised to stroke him every day.

However, I anticipate. As soon as the secretarial life was saved, Margery said "Agga," which is, as it were, "*Encore!*" or "*Bis!*" so that I have her permission to tell you that story all over again. Indeed, I should feel quite justified in doing so. Instead I will give you the tragedy of George, the other fellow (no knight he), as she told it to me afterwards.

"George was quite a different man from Sir Arthur. So far from being elected to anything under Rule Two, he got blackballed for the St John's Wood Toilet Club. Opinions differed as to why this happened; some said it was his personal unpopularity (he had previously been up, without success, for membership of the local Ratepayers Association); others (among them the proprietor), that his hair grew too quickly. Anyhow, it was a great shock to George, and they had to have a man in to break it to him. (It's always the way when you have a man in.)

"George was stricken to the heart. This last blow was too much for what had always been a proud nature. He decided to emigrate. Accordingly he left home, and moved to Kilburn. Whether he is still there or not I cannot say; but a card with that postmark reached his niece only this week. It was unsigned, and bore on the space reserved for inland communications these words: *The old old wish — A Merry Christmas and a Happy New Year.*"

"But what about the javelin?" I asked Margery. (This fellow had a javelin too, you remember.)

"*Gorky*," said Margery, for the third time which means—

Well, upon my word, I don't know what it means. But it would explain it all.

Meanwhile, Sir Arthur (he was in my story, you know) is still waiting for the secretary. In case the butter gives out, have I mentioned that the secretary wants all the flowers to be white?

THE ART OF CONVERSATION

"In conversation," said somebody (I think it was my grandfather), "there should always be a give and take. The ball must be kept rolling." If he had ever had a niece two years old, I don't think he would have bothered.

"What's 'at?" said Margery, pointing suddenly.

"That," I said, stroking it, "is dear uncle's nose."

"What's 'at?"

"Take your finger away. Ah, yes, that is dear uncle's eye. The left one."

"Dear uncle's left one," said Margery thoughtfully. "What's it doing?"

"Thinking."

"What's finking?"

"What dear uncle does every afternoon after lunch."

"What's lunch?"

"Eggs, sardines, macaroons—everything."

With a great effort Margery resisted the temptation to ask what "everything" was (a difficult question), or what everything was doing (a still more difficult one), and made a statement of her own.

"Santa Claus bring Margie a balloon from daddy," she announced.

"A balloon! How jolly!" I said with interest. "What sort are you having? One of those semi-detached ones with the gas laid on, or the pink ones with a velvet collar?"

"Down chimney," said Margery.

"Oh, *that* kind. Do you think—I mean, isn't it rather——"

"Tell Margie a story about a balloon."

"Bother," I murmured.

"What's bovver?"

"Bother is what you say when relations ask you to tell them a story about a balloon. It means, 'But for the fact that we both have the Montmorency blood in our veins, I should be compelled to decline your kind invitation, all the stories I know about balloons being stiff 'uns.' It also means, 'Instead of talking about balloons, won't you sing me a little song?'"

"Nope," said Margery.

"Bother, she's forgotten her music."

"What did you say, uncle dear, what did you say?"

I sighed and began.

"Once upon a time there was a balloon, a dear little toy balloon, and—and——"

"What's 'at?" asked Margery, making a dab at my chest. "What's 'at, uncle dear?"

"That," I said, "is a button. More particularly, a red waistcoat button. More particularly still, my top red waistcoat button."

"What's 'at?" she asked, going down one.

"That is a button. *Description*: second, red, waistcoat. *Parents living*: both. *Injections diseases*: scarlet fever slightly once."

"What's 'at?"

"That's a—ah, yes, a button. The third. A good little chap, but not so chubby as his brothers. He couldn't go down to Margate with them last year, and so, of course—— Well, as I was saying, there was once a balloon, and——"

"What's 'a-a-at?" said Margery, bending forward suddenly and kissing it.

"Look here, you've jolly well got to enclose a stamped addressed envelope with the next question. As a matter of fact, though you won't believe me, that again is a button."

"What's 'at?" asked Margery, digging at the fifth button.

"Owing to extreme pressure on space," I began.... "Thank you. That also is a button. Its responsibility is greater than that of its brethren. The crash may come at any moment. Luckily it has booked its passage to the—— Where was I? Oh yes—well, this balloon——"

"What's 'at?" said Margery, pointing to the last one.

"I must have written notice of that question. I can't tell you offhand."

"What's 'at, uncle dear?"

"Well, I don't know, Margie. It looks something like a collar stud, only somehow you wouldn't expect to find a collar-stud there. Of course it may have slipped.... Or could it be one of those red beads, do you think? N-no, no, it isn't a bead.... And it isn't a raspberry; because this is the wrong week for raspberries. Of course it might be a — — By Jove, I've got it! It's a button!"

I gave the sort of war-whoop with which one announces these discoveries, and Margery whooped too.

"A button!" she cried. "A dear little button!" She thought for a moment. "What's a button?"

This was ridiculous.

"You don't mean to say," I reproached her, "that I've got to tell you now what a button is? *That,*" I added severely, pointing to the top of my waistcoat, "is a button."

"What's 'at?" said Margery, pointing to the next one.

I looked at her in horror. Then I began to talk very quickly.

"There was once a balloon," I said rapidly, "a dear little boy balloon, I mean toy balloon, and this balloon was a jolly little balloon just two minutes old, and he wasn't always asking silly questions, and when he fell down and exploded himself they used to wring him out and say, 'Come, come, now, be a little airship about it,' and so — —"

"What's 'at?" asked Margery, pointing to the top button.

There was only one way out of it. I began to sing a carol in a very shrill voice.

All the artist rose in Margery.

"Don't sing," she said hurriedly. "Margie sing. What will Margie sing, uncle?"

Before I could suggest anything, she was off. It was a scandalous song. She began by announcing that she wanted to be among the boys, and (guessing that I should object) assured me that it was no good kicking up a noise, because it was no fun going out when there weren't any boys about, you were so lonely-onely-onely ...

Here the tune became undecided; and, a chance word recalling another context to her mind, she drifted suddenly into a hymn, and sang it with the same religious fervour as she had sung the other, her fair head flung back and her hazel eyes gazing into heaven ...

I listened carefully. This was a bit I didn't recognise.... The tune wavered for a moment ... and out of it these words emerged triumphant,

"Talk of me to the boys you meet,
Remember me kindly to Regent Street,
And give them my love in the— —"

"What's 'at, uncle?"

"That," I said, stroking it, "is dear uncle's nose."

"What's— —"

By the way, would you like it all over again? No? Oh, very well.

AFTERNOON SLEEP

"In the afternoon they came unto a land
In which it seemed always afternoon."

I am like Napoleon in that I can go to sleep at any moment; I am unlike him (I believe) in that I am always doing so. One makes no apology for doing so on Sunday afternoon—the apology, indeed, should come from the others, the wakeful parties.

"Uncle?"

"Margery."

"Will you come and play wiv me?"

"I'm rather busy just now," I said, with closed eyes. "After tea."

"Why are you raver busy just now? My baby's only raver busy sometimes."

"Well, then, you know what it's like; how important it is that one shouldn't be disturbed."

"But you must be beturbed when I ask you to come and play wiv me."

"Oh, well ... what shall we play at?"

"Trains," said Margery eagerly.

When we play trains I have to be a tunnel. I don't know if you have ever been a tunnel? No; well, it's an over-rated profession.

"We won't play trains," I announced firmly, "because it's Sunday."

"Why not because it's Sunday?"

(Oh, you little pagan!)

"Hasn't mummy told you all about Sunday?"

"Oh yes, Maud did tell me," said Margery casually. Then she gave an innocent little smile. "Oh, I called mummy Maud," she said in pretended surprise. "I quite *fought* I was upstairs!"

I hope you follow. The manners and customs of good society must be observed on the ground floor where visitors may happen; upstairs one relaxes a little.

"Do you know," Margery went on with the air of a discoverer, "you mustn't say 'prayers' downstairs. Or 'corsets.'"

"I never do," I affirmed. "Well, anyhow I never will again."

"Why mayn't you?"

"I don't know," I said sleepily.

"Say prehaps."

"Well—*prehaps* it's because your mother tells you not to."

"Well, 'at's a *silly* fing to say," said Margery scornfully.

"It is. I'm thoroughly ashamed of it. I apologise. Good-night." And I closed my eyes again.

"I fought you were going to play wiv me, Mr Bingle," sighed Margery to herself.

"My name is *not* Bingle," I said, opening one eye.

"Why isn't it Bingle?"

"The story is a very long and sad one. When I wake up I will tell it to you. Good-night."

"Tell it to me now."

There was no help for it.

"Once upon a time," I said rapidly, "there was a man called Bingle, Oliver Bingle, and he married a lady called Pringle. And his brother married a lady called Jingle. And his other brother married a Miss Wingle. And his cousin remained single.... That is all."

"Oh, I see," said Margery doubtfully. "Now will you play wiv me?"

How can one resist the pleading of a young cheild?

"All right," I said. "We'll pretend I'm a little girl, and you're my mummy, and you've just put me to bed.... Good-night, mummy dear."

"Oh, but I must cover you up." She fetched a tablecloth, and a pram-cover, and *The Times*, and a handkerchief, and the cat, and a doll's what-I-mustn't-say-downstairs, and a cushion; and she covered me up and tucked me in.

"'Ere, 'ere, now go to sleep, my darling," she said, and kissed me lovingly.

"Oh, Margie, you dear," I whispered.

"You called me 'Margie'!" she cried in horror.

"I meant 'Mummy.' Good-night."

One, two, three seconds passed rapidly.

"It's morning," said a bright voice in my ear. "Get up."

"I'm very ill," I pleaded; "I want to stay in bed all day."

"But your dear uncle," said Margery, inventing hastily, "came last night after you were in bed, and stayed 'e night. Do you see? And he wants you to sit on his chest in bed and talk to him."

"Where is he? Show me the bounder."

"'Ere he is," said Margery, pointing at me.

"But look here, I can't sit on my own chest and talk to myself. I'll take the two parts if you insist, Sir Herbert, but I can't play them simultaneously. Not even Irving——"

"Why can't you play vem simrulaleously?"

"Well, I can't. Margie, *will* you let me go to sleep?"

"Nope," said Margery, shaking her head.

"You should say, 'No, thank you, revered and highly respected uncle.'"

"No *hank* you, Mr Cann."

"I have already informed you that my name is not Bingle; and I have now to add that neither is it Cann."

"Why neiver is it Cann?"

"That isn't grammar. You should say, 'Why can it not either?'"

"Why?"

"I don't know."

"Say prehaps."

"No, I can't even say prehaps."

"Well, say I shall understand when I'm a big girl."

"You'll understand when you're a big girl, Margery," I said solemnly.

"Oh, I see."

"That's right. Now then, what about going to sleep?"

She was silent for a moment, and I thought I was safe. Then— —

"Uncle, just tell me—why was 'at little boy crying vis morning?"

"Which little boy?"

"Ve one in 'e road."

"Oh, that one. Well, he was crying because his uncle hadn't had any sleep all night, and when he tried to go to sleep in the afternoon— —"

"Say prehaps again."

My first rejected contribution! I sighed and had another shot. "Well, then," I said gallantly, "it must have been because he hadn't got a sweet little girl of three to play with him."

"Yes," said Margery, nodding her head thoughtfully, "'at was it."

TO JOCK

(ON CHOOSING A PROFESSION)

When, Jock, I saw you, debonair and bland,
Shin perilously up the cottage grand
Piano, with the bread-knife in your hand;—

When I observed your friendly little stare,
Your guileless baby face, your general air
Of "Golly, how on earth did I get *there*?" —

When I remarked how cheerfully you crashed
Down on the tea-things, not the least abashed
To see the same (*my* wedding present) *smashed*!—

Then as we wondered (having wiped the tea
From off this waistcoat) "What's he going to be?"
I knew at once why father thought, "The sea."

There are who sit and languidly dictate
Letters beginning "Yours of even date" —
Each one designed to rope in six-and-eight;

Wherefore each letter carefully postpones
The moment when the other party owns
His case is badly dished by "*Rex v. Jones.*"

There are who daily in the safe retreat
Of some Department gather round and bleat
Scandal and Art, until it's time to eat;

Return at three, and, having written "Dear
Sir, your communication of last year
Duly received and noted"—disappear.

There are who do not hesitate to shove
Their views of Babes and Budgets, Life and Love
On paper—as it might be up above;

Who, fearless fellows, are not found to flinch
When some Proprietor essays to pinch
Their holiest thoughts at eightpence for the inch.

Such, Jock, as these are we who bear your name
Content (well, almost) with the good old game
Of moderate Fortune unrelieved by Fame.

But there are Nobler Souls about the place,
Such spirits as have built our Island Race,
Heroes who must, who simply must, have *space*.

'Twas not to serve the pen that Nature gave
To these their love of all that's large and brave;
For Them an ampler life upon the Wave!

So when your father (while I mop the tea)
Says that he rather thinks you'll go to sea,
Dear Jock, sweet Jock, your uncle *must* agree.

MORE CRICKET

TO AN OLD BAT

When Vesper trails her gown of grey
Across the lawn at six or seven
The diligent observer may
(Or may) see, athwart the heaven,
An aimless rodent on the wing. Well, that
Is (probably) a Bat....
In any case I shall not sing of that.

O Willow, in our hours of ease
    (That is to say, throughout the Winter),
I take you sometimes on my knees,
    And careless of the frequent splinter,
Caress you tenderly, and sigh, and say,
    "Ye Gods, how long till May?"

And so as soon as April's here
    I do not sob for Spring to show its
Pale daffodils and all the dear
    Old flowers that keep the minor poets;
I sing it just because a month (about)
    Will find you fairly out.

Revered, beloved, O you whose job
    Is but to serve throughout the season—
To make, if so it be, the Blob,
    And not (thank heaven!) to ask the reason—
To stand, like Mrs Hemans' little friend,
    Undoubting to the end:

Old Willow, what a tale to tell—
    Our steady rise, from small beginnings,
*Ab ovo usque—usque—*well,
    To eighty-four, our highest innings;

(Ah me, that crowded hour of glorious lives—
    Ten of them, all from drives!)

Once only have you let me in,
    Through all the knocks we've had together;
That time when, wanting four to win,
    I fairly tried to tonk the leather—
And lo! a full-faced welt, without the least
    Warning, went S.S.E.

A painful scene. In point of fact
    I'm doubtful if I ought to hymn it;
Enough to say you went and cracked,
    And left me thinking things like "Dimmit"
(And not like "Dimmit"), as I heard Slip call
    "Mine!" and he pouched the ball.

Do you remember, too, the game
    One August somewhere down in Dorset
When, being told to force the same,
    We straightway started in to force it....
For half-an-hour or so we saw it through,
    And scratched a priceless two;

Or how the prayer to play for keeps
    And hang the runs, we didn't need 'em,
So stirred us, we collected heaps
    With rather more than usual freedom;
Fifteen in fourteen minutes—till a catch
    Abruptly closed the match?

Well, well—the coming years (if fine)
    Shall see us going even stronger;
So pouring out the oil and wine,
    Let's sit and drink, a little longer;
Here's to a decent average of ten!
    (Yours is the oil. Say when....)

When Morning on the heels of Night
    Picks up her shroud at five and after,
The diffident observer might
    (Or might not) see, beneath a rafter,
A pensive rodent upside down. Well, that
    Is (possibly) a Bat....
In any case I have not sung of that.

A SCRATCH LOT

I. THE CHOOSING OF THE DAY

As soon as I had promised to take an eleven down to Chartleigh I knew that I was in for trouble; but I did not realise how great it would be until I consulted Henry Barton. Henry is a first-class cricketer, and it was my idea that he should do all the batting for us, and such of the bowling as the laws allowed. I had also another idea, and this I explained to Henry.

"As you are aware," I said, "the ideal side contains five good bats, four good bowlers, a wicket-keeper, and Henry Barton."

"Quite so," agreed Henry.

"That is the principle on which one selects an eleven. Now, I intend to strike out a line of my own. My team shall consist of three authors or journalists, two solicitors, four barristers, a couple from the Stock Exchange, some civil servants and an artist or two. How many is that?"

"Nineteen."

"Well, that's the idea, anyhow."

"It's a rotten idea."

"No, it's a splendid idea. I wonder nobody has thought of it before. I send a solicitor and a journalist in first. The journalist uses the long handle, while the solicitor plays for keeps."

"And where does the artist come in?"

"The artist comes in last, and plays for a draw. You are very slow today, Henry."

Henry, the man of leisure, thought a moment.

"Yes, that's all very well for you working men," he said at last, "but what do I go as? Or am I one of the barristers?"

"You go as 'with Barton.' Yes. If you're very good you shall have an 'H' in brackets after you. 'With Barton (H)'"

The method of choosing my team being settled, the next thing was the day. "Any day in the first week in July," the Chartleigh captain had said. Now at first sight there appear to be seven days in the week, but it is not really so. For instance, Saturday. Now there's a good day! What could one object to in a Saturday?

But do you imagine Henry Barton would let it pass?

"I don't think you'll get eleven people for the Saturday," he said. "People are always playing cricket on Saturday."

"Precisely," I said. "Healthy exercise for the London toiler. That's why I'm asking 'em."

"But I mean they'll have arranged to play already with their own teams. Or else they'll be going away for week-ends."

"One can spend a very pretty week-end at Chartleigh."

"H'm, let me think. Any day in the week, isn't it?"

"Except, apparently, Saturday," I said huffily.

"Let's see now, what days are there?"

I mentioned two or three of the better-known ones.

"Yes. Of course, some of those are impossible, though. We'd better go through the week and see which is best."

I don't know who Barton is that he should take it upon himself to make invidious distinctions between the days of the week.

"Very well, then," I said. "Sunday."

"Ass."

That seemed to settle Sunday, so we passed on to Monday.

"You won't get your stockbroker on Monday," said Henry. "It's Contanger day or something with them every Monday."

"Stocktaking, don't you mean?"

"I dare say. Anyhow, no one in the House can get away on a Monday."

"I must have my stockbrokers. Tuesday."

Tuesday, it seemed, was hopeless. I was a fool to have thought of Tuesday. Why, everybody knew that Tuesday was an impossible day for——

I forget what spoilt Tuesday's chance. I fancy it was a busy day for Civil Servants. No one in the Home Civil can get away on a Tuesday. I know that sounds absurd, but Henry was being absurd just then. Or was it barristers? Briefs get given out on a Tuesday, I was made to understand. That brought us to Wednesday. I hoped much from Wednesday.

"Yes," said Henry. "Wednesday might do. Of course most of the weeklies go to press on Wednesday. Rather an awkward day for journalists. What about Thursday?"

I began to get annoyed.

"Thursday my flannel trousers go to the press," I said—"that is to say, they come back from the wash then."

"Look here, why try to be funny?"

"Hang it, who started it? Talking about Contanger-days. Contanger—it sounds like a new kind of guano."

"Well, if you don't believe me— —"

"Henry, I do. Thursday be it, then."

"Yes, I suppose that's all right," said Henry doubtfully.

"Why not? Don't say it's sending-in day with artists," I implored. "Not *every* Thursday?"

"No. Only there's Friday, and— —"

"Friday is *my* busy day," I pleaded—"my one ewe lamb. Do not rob me of it."

"It's a very good day, Friday. I think you'd find that most people could get off then."

"But why throw over Thursday like this? A good, honest day, Henry. Many people get born on a Thursday, Henry. And it's a marrying day, Henry. A nice, clean, sober day, and you— —"

"The fact is," said Henry, "I've suddenly remembered I'm engaged myself on Thursday."

This was too much.

"Henry," I said coldly, "you forget yourself—you forget yourself strangely, my lad. Just because I was weak enough to promise you an 'H' after your name. You seem to have forgotten that the 'H' was to be in brackets."

"Yes, but I'm afraid I really am engaged."

"Are you really? Look here—I'll leave out the 'with' and you shall be one of us. There! Baby, see the pretty gentlemen!"

Henry smiled and shook his head.

"Oh, well," I said, "we must have you. So if you say Friday, Friday it is. You're quite sure Friday is all right for solicitors? Very well, then."

So the day was settled for Friday. It was rather a pity, because, as I said, in the ordinary way Friday is the day I put aside for work.

II. THE SELECTION COMMITTEE

The committee consisted of Henry and myself. Originally it was myself alone, but as soon as I had selected Henry I proceeded to co-opt him, reserving to myself, however, the right of a casting vote in case of any difference of opinion. One arose, almost immediately, over Higgins. Henry said:

(*a*) That Higgins had once made ninety-seven.

(*b*) That he had been asked to play for his county.

(*c*) That he was an artist, and we had arranged to have an artist in the team.

In reply I pointed out:

(*a*) That ninety-seven was an extremely unlikely number for anyone to have made.

(*b*) That if he had been asked he evidently hadn't accepted, which showed the sort of man he was: besides which, what was his county?

(*c*) That, assuming for the moment he had made ninety-seven, was it likely he would consent to go in last and play for a draw, which was why we wanted the artist? And that, anyhow, he was a jolly bad artist.

(d) That hadn't we better put it to the vote?

This was accordingly done, and an exciting division ended in a tie.

Those in favour of Higgins   1
Those against Higgins   1

The Speaker gave his casting vote against Higgins.

Prior to this, however, I had laid before the House the letter of invitation. It was as follows (and, I flatter myself, combined tact with a certain dignity): —

"DEAR——, I am taking a team into the country on Friday week to play against the village eleven. The ground and the lunch are good. Do you think you could manage to come down? I know you are very busy just now with

Contangers,
Briefs,
Clients,
Your Christmas Number,
Varnishing Day,
(*Strike out all but one of these*)

but a day in the country would do you good. I hear from all sides that you are in great form this season. I will give you all particulars about trains later on. Good-bye. Remember me to— —. How is— —? Ever yours.

"*P.S.*—Old Henry is playing for us. He has strained himself a little and probably won't bowl much, so I expect we shall all have a turn with the ball."

Or, "I don't think you have ever met Henry Barton, the cricketer. He is very keen on meeting you. Apparently he has seen you play somewhere. He will be turning out for us on Friday.

"*P.P.S.*—We might manage to have some bridge in the train."

"That," I said to Henry, "is what I call a clever letter."

"What makes you think that?"

"It is all clever," I said modestly. "But the cleverest part is a sentence at the end. 'I will give you all particulars about trains later on.' You see I have been looking them up, and we leave Victoria at seven-thirty A.M. and get back to London Bridge at eleven-forty-five P.M."

The answers began to come in the next day. One of the first was from Bolton, the solicitor, and it upset us altogether. For, after accepting the invitation, he went on: "I am afraid I don't play bridge. As you may remember, I used to play chess at Cambridge, and I still keep it up."

"Chess," said Henry. "That's where White plays and mates in two moves. And there's a Black too. He does something."

"We shall have to get a Black. This is awful."

"Perhaps Bolton would like to do problems by himself all the time."

"That would be rather bad luck on him. No, look here. Here's Carey. Glad to come, but doesn't bridge. He's the man."

Accordingly we wired to Carey: "Do you play chess? Reply at once." He answered, "No. Why?"

"Carey will have to play that game with glass balls. Solitaire. Yes. We must remember to bring a board with us."

"But what about the chess gentleman?" asked Henry.

"I must go and find one. We've had one refusal."

There is an editor I know slightly, so I called upon him at his office. I found him writing verses.

"Be brief," he said, "I'm frightfully busy."

"I have just three questions to ask you," I replied.

"What rhymes with 'yorker'?"

"That wasn't one of them."

"Yorker—corker—por——"

"Better make it a full pitch," I suggested. "Step out and make it a full pitch. Then there are such lots of rhymes."

"Thanks, I will. Well?"

"One. Do you play bridge?"

"No."

"Two. Do you play chess?"

"I can."

"Three. Do you play cricket? Not that it matters."

"Yes, I do sometimes. Good-bye. Send me a proof, will you? By the way, what paper is this for?"

"*The Sportsman*, if you'll play. On Friday week. Do."

"Anything, if you'll go."

"May I have that in writing?"

He handed me a rejection form.

"There you are. And I'll do anything you like on Friday."

I went back to Henry and told him the good news.

"I wonder if he'll mind being black," said Henry. "That's the chap that always gets mated so quickly."

"I expect they'll arrange it among themselves. Anyhow, we've done our best for them."

"It's an awful business, getting up a team," said Henry thoughtfully. "Well, we shall have two decent sets of bridge, anyway. But you ought to have arranged for twelve aside, and then we could have left out the chess professors and had three sets."

"It's all the fault of the rules. Some day somebody will realise that four doesn't go into eleven, and then we shall have a new rule."

"No, I don't think so," said Henry. "I don't fancy 'Wanderer' would allow it."

III. IN THE TRAIN

If there is one thing I cannot stand, it is ingratitude. Take the case of Carey. Carey, you may remember, professed himself unable to play either bridge or chess; and as we had a three-hour journey before us it did not look as though he were going to have much of a time. However, Henry and I, thinking entirely of Carey's personal comfort, went to the trouble of buying him a solitaire board, with glass balls complete. The balls were all in different colours.

I laid this before Carey as soon as we settled in the train.

"Whatever's that?"

"The new game," I said. "It's all the rage now, the man tells me. The Smart Set play it every Sunday. Young girls are inveigled into lonely country houses and robbed of incredible sums."

Carey laughed scornfully.

"So it is alleged," I added. "The inventor claims for it that in some respects it has advantages which even cricket cannot claim. As, for instance, it can be played in any weather: nay, even upon the sick bed."

"And how exactly is it played?"

"Thus. You take one away and all the rest jump over each other. At each jump you remove the jumpee, and the object is to clear the board. Hence the name—solitaire."

"I see. It seems a pretty rotten game."

That made me angry.

"All right. Then don't play. Have a game of marbles on the rack instead."

Meanwhile Henry was introducing Bolton and the editor to each other.

"Two such famous people," he began.

"Everyone," said Bolton, with a bow, "knows the editor of— —"

"Oh yes, there's that. But I meant two such famous chess players. Bolton," he explained to the editor, "was twelfth man against Oxford some years ago. Something went wrong with his heart, or he'd have got in. On his day, and if the board was at all sticky, he used to turn a good deal from QB4."

"Do you really play?" asked Bolton eagerly. "I have a board here."

"Does he play! Do you mean to say you have never heard of the Trocadero Defence?"

"The Sicilian Defence——"

"The Trocadero Defence. It's where you palm the other man's queen when he's not looking. Most effective opening."

They both seemed keen on beginning, so Henry got out the cards for the rest of us.

I drew the younger journalist, against Henry and the senior stockbroker. Out of compliment to the journalist we arranged to play half-a-crown a hundred, that being about the price they pay him. I dealt, and a problem arose immediately. Here it is.

"A deals and leaves it to his partner B, who goes No Trumps. Y leads a small heart. B's hand consists of king and three small diamonds, king and one other heart, king and three small clubs, and three small spades. A plays the king from Dummy, and Z puts on the ace. What should A do?"

Answer. Ring communication-cord and ask guard to remove B.

"Very well," I said to Dummy. "One thing's pretty clear. You don't bowl to-day. Long-leg both ends is about your mark. Somewhere where there's plenty of throwing to do."

Later on, when I was Dummy, I strolled over to the chess players.

"What's the ground like?" said the editor, as he finessed a knight.

"Sporting. Distinctly sporting."

"Long grass all round, I suppose?"

"Oh, lord, no. The cows eat up all that."

"Do you mean to say the cows are allowed on the pitch?"

"Well, they don't put it that way, quite. The pitch is allowed on the cows' pasture land."

"I suppose if we make a hundred we shall do well?" asked somebody.

"If we make fifty we shall declare," I said. "By Jove, Bolton, that's a pretty smart move."

I may not know all the technical terms, but I do understand the idea of chess. The editor was a pawn up and three to play, and had just advanced his queen against Bolton's king, putting on a lot of check side as it seemed to me. Of course, I expected Bolton would have to retire his king; but not he! He laid a stymie with his bishop, and it was the editor's queen that had to withdraw. Yet Bolton was only spare man at Cambridge!

"I am not at all sure," I said, "that chess is not a finer game even than solitaire."

"It's a finer game than cricket," said Bolton, putting his bishop back in the slips again.

"No," said the editor. "Cricket is the finest game in the world. For why? I will tell you."

"Thanks to the glorious uncertainty of our national pastime," began the journalist, from his next Monday's article.

"No, thanks to the fact that it is a game in which one can produce the maximum of effect with the minimum of skill. Take my own case. I am not a batsman, I shall never make ten runs in an innings, yet how few people realise that! I go in first wicket down, wearing my M.C.C. cap. Having taken guard with the help of a bail, I adopt Palairet's stance at the wicket. Then the bowler delivers: either to the off, to leg, or straight. If it is to the off, I shoulder my bat and sneer at it. If it is to leg, I swing at it. I have a beautiful swing, which is alone worth the money. Probably I miss, but the bowler fully understands that it is because I have not yet got the pace of the wicket. Sooner or later he sends down a straight one, whereupon I proceed to glide it to leg. You will see the stroke in Beldam's book. Of course, I miss the ball, and am given out l.b.w. Then the look of astonishment that passes over my face, the bewildered inquiry of the wicket-keeper, and finally the shrug of good-humoured resignation as I walk from the crease! Nine times out of ten square-leg asks the umpire what county I play for. That is cricket."

"Quite so," I said, when he had finished. "There's only one flaw in it. That is that quite possibly you may have to go in last to-day. You'll have to think of some other plan. Also on this wicket the ball always goes well over your head. You couldn't be l.b.w. if you tried."

"Oh, but I do try."

"Yes. Well, you'll find it difficult."

The editor sighed.

"Then I shall have to retire hurt," he said.

Bolton chuckled to himself.

"One never retires hurt at chess," he said, as he huffed the editor's king. "Though once," he added proudly, "I sprained my hand, and had to make all my moves with the left one. Check."

The editor yawned, and looked out of the window.

"Are we nearly there?" he asked.

IV. IN THE FIELD

It is, I consider, the duty of a captain to consult the wishes of his team now and then, particularly when he is in command of such a heterogeneous collection of the professions as I was. I was watching a match at the Oval once, and at the end of an over Lees went up to Dalmeny, and had a few words with him. Probably, I thought, he is telling him a good story that he heard at lunch; or, maybe, he is asking for the latest gossip from the Lobby. My neighbour, however, held other views.

"There," he said, "there's ole Walter Lees asking to be took off."

"Surely not," I answered. "Dalmeny had a telegram just now, and Lees is asking if it's the three-thirty winner."

Lees then began to bowl again.

"There you are," I said triumphantly, but my neighbour wouldn't hear of it.

"Ole Lees asked to be took off, and ole Dalmeny" (I forget how he pronounced it, but I know it was one of the wrong ways)—"ole Dalmeny told him he'd have to stick on a bit."

Now that made a great impression on me, and I agreed with my friend that Dalmeny was in the wrong.

"When I am captaining a team," I said, "and one of the bowlers wants to come off, I am always ready to meet him half-way, more than half-way. Better than that, if I have resolved upon any course of action, I always let my team know beforehand; and I listen to their objections in a fair-minded spirit."

It was in accordance with this rule of mine that I said casually, as we were changing, "If we win the toss I shall put them in."

There was a chorus of protest.

"That's right, go it," I said. "Henry objects because, as a first-class cricketer, he is afraid of what *The Sportsman* will say if we lose. The editor naturally objects—it ruins his chance of being mistaken for a county player if he has to field first. Bolton objects because heavy exercise on a hot day spoils his lunch. Thompson objects because that's the way he earns his living at the Bar. His objection is merely technical, and is reserved as a point of law for the Court of Crown Cases Reserved. Markham is a socialist and objects to authority. Also he knows he's got to field long-leg both ends. Gerald——"

"But why?" said Henry.

"Because I want you all to see the wicket first. Then you can't say you weren't warned." Whereupon I went out and lost the toss.

As we walked into the field the editor told me a very funny story. I cannot repeat it here for various reasons. First, it has nothing to do with cricket; and, secondly, it is, I understand, coming out in his next number, and I should probably get into trouble. Also it is highly technical, and depends largely for its success upon adequate facial expression. But it amused me a good deal. Just as he got to the exciting part, Thompson came up.

"Do you mind if I go cover?" he asked.

"Do," I said abstractedly. "And what did the vicar say?"

The editor chuckled. "Well, you see, the vicar, knowing, of course, that——"

"Cover, I suppose," said Gerald, as he caught us up.

"What? Oh yes, please. The vicar did know, did he?"

"Oh, the vicar *knew*. That's really the whole point."

I shouted with laughter.

"Good, isn't it?" said the editor. "Well, then——"

"Have you got a cover?" came Markham's voice from behind us.

I turned round.

"Oh, Markham," I said, "I shall want you cover, if you don't mind. Sorry—I must tell these men where to go—well, then, you were saying——"

The editor continued the story. We were interrupted once or twice, but he finished it just as their first two men came out. I particularly liked that bit about the——

"Jove," I said suddenly, "we haven't got a wicket-keeper. That's always the way. Can you keep?" I asked the editor.

"Isn't there anyone else?"

"I'm afraid they're all fielding cover," I said, remembering suddenly. "But, look here, it's the chance of a lifetime for you. You can tell 'em all that——"

But he was trotting off to the pavilion.

"Can anybody lend me some gloves?" he asked. "They want me to keep wicket. Thing I've never done in my life. Of course I always field cover in the ordinary way. Thanks awfully. Sure you don't mind? Don't suppose I shall stop a ball though."

"Henry," I called, "you're starting that end. Arrange the field, will you? I'll go cover. You're sure to want one."

Their first batsman was an old weather-beaten villager called George. We knew his name was George because the second ball struck him in the stomach and his partner said, "Stay there, George," which seemed to be George's idea too. We learnt at lunch that once, in the eighties or so, he had gone in first with Lord Hawke (which put him on a level with that player), and that he had taken first ball (which put him just above the Yorkshireman).

There the story ended, so far as George was concerned; and indeed it was enough. Why seek to inquire if George took any other balls besides the first?

In our match, however, he took the second in the place that I mentioned, the third on the back of the neck, the fourth on the elbow, and the fifth in the original place; while the sixth, being off the wicket, was left there. Nearly every batsman had some pet stroke, and we soon saw that George's stroke was the leg-bye. His bat was the second line of defence, and was kept well in the block. If the ball escaped the earthwork in front, there was always a chance that it would be brought up by the bat. Once, indeed, a splendid ball of Henry's which came with his arm and missed George's legs, snicked the bat, and went straight into the wicket-keeper's hands. The editor, however, presented his compliments, and regretted that he was unable to accept the enclosed, which he accordingly returned with many thanks.

There was an unwritten law that George could not be l.b.w. I cannot say how it arose—possibly from a natural coyness on George's part about the exact significance of the "l." Henry, after appealing for the best part of three overs, gave it up, and bowled what he called "googlies" at him. This looked more hopeful, because a googly seems in no way to be restricted as to the number of its bounces, and at each bounce it had a chance of doing something. Unfortunately it never did George. Lunch came and the score was thirty-seven—George having compiled in two hours a masterly nineteen; eighteen off the person, but none the less directly due to him.

"We must think of a plan of campaign at lunch," said Henry. "It's hopeless to go on like this."

"Does George drink?" I asked anxiously. It seemed the only chance.

But George didn't. And the score was thirty seven for five, which is a good score for the wicket.

V. AT THE WICKETS

At lunch I said: "I have just had a wire from the Surrey committee to say that I may put myself on to bowl."

"That is good hearing," said Henry.

"Did they hear?" asked Gerald anxiously, looking over at the Chartleigh team.

"You may think you're very funny, but I'll bet you a—a—anything you like that I get George out."

"All right," said Gerald. "I'll play you for second wicket down, the loser to go in last."

"Done," I said, "and what about passing the salad now?"

After lunch the editor took me on one side and said: "I don't like it. I don't like it at all."

"Then why did you have so much?" I asked.

"I mean the wicket. It's dangerous. I am not thinking of myself so much as of— —"

"As of the reading public?"

"Quite so."

"You think you—you would be missed in Fleet Street—just at first?"

"You are not putting the facts too strongly. I was about to suggest that I should be a 'did not bat.'"

"Oh! I see. Perhaps I ought to tell you that I was talking just now to the sister of their captain."

The editor looked interested.

"About the pad of the gardener?" he said.

"About you. She said—I give you her own words—'Who is the tall, handsome man keeping wicket in a M.C.C. cap?' So I said you were a well-known county player, as she would see when you went in to bat."

The editor shook my hand impressively.

"Thank you very much," he said. "I shall not fail her. What county did you say?"

"Part of Flint. You know the little bit that's got into the wrong county by mistake? That part. She had never heard of it; but I assured her it had a little bit of yellow all to itself on the map. Have you a pretty good eleven?"

The editor swore twice—once for me and once for Flint. Then we went out into the field.

My first ball did for George. I followed the tactics of William the First at the Battle of Hastings, 1066. You remember how he ordered his archers to shoot into the air, and how one arrow fell and pierced the eye of Harold, whereupon confusion and disaster arose. So with George. I hurled one perpendicularly into the sky, and it dropped (after a long time) straight upon the batsman. George followed it with a slightly contemptuous eye... all the way....

All the way. Of course, I was sorry. We were all much distressed. They told us afterwards he had never been hit in the eye before.... One gets new experiences.

George retired hurt. Not so much hurt as piqued, I fancy. He told the umpire it wasn't bowling. Possibly. Neither was it batting. It was just superior tactics.

The innings soon closed, and we had sixty-one to win, and, what seemed more likely, fifty-nine and various other numbers to lose. Sixty-one is a very unlucky number with me—oddly enough I have never yet made sixty-one; like W.G. Grace, who had never made ninety-three. My average this season is five, which is a respectable number. As Bolton pointed out—if we each got five to-day, and there were six extras, we should win. I suppose if one plays chess a good deal one thinks of these things.

Harold, I mean George, refused to field, so I nobly put myself in last and substituted for him. This was owing to an argument as to the exact wording of my bet with Gerald.

"You said you'd get him out," said Gerald.

"I mean 'out of the way,' 'out of the field,' 'out of——'"

"I meant 'out' according to the laws of cricket. There are nine ways. Which was yours, I should like to know?"

"Obstructing the ball."

"There you are."

I shifted my ground.

"I didn't say I'd get him out," I explained. "I said I'd get him. Those were my very words. 'I will get George.' Can you deny that I got him?"

"Even if you said that, which you didn't, the common construction that one puts upon the phrase is——"

"If you are going to use long words like that," I said, "I must refer you to my solicitor Bolton."

Whereupon Bolton took counsel's opinion, and reported that he could not advise me to proceed in the matter. So Gerald took second wicket, and I fielded.

However, one advantage of fielding was that I saw the editor's innings from start to finish at the closest quarters. He came in at the end of the first over, and took guard for "left hand round the wicket."

"Would you give it me?" he said to Bolton. "These country umpires.... Thanks. And what's that over the wicket? Thanks."

He marked two places with the bail.

"How about having it from here?" I suggested at mid-on. "It's quite a good place and we're in a straight line with the church."

The editor returned the bail, and held up his bat again.

"That 'one-leg' all right? Thanks."

He was proceeding to look round the field when a gentle voice from behind him said: "If you wouldn't mind moving a bit, sir, I could bowl."

"Oh, is it over?" said the editor airily, trying to hide his confusion. "I beg your pardon, I beg your pardon."

Still he had certainly impressed the sister of their captain, and it was dreadful to think of the disillusionment that might follow at any moment. However, as it happened, he had yet another trick up his sleeve. Bolton hit a ball to cover, and the editor, in the words of the local paper, "most sportingly sacrificed his wicket when he saw that his partner had not time to get back. It was a question, however, whether there was ever a run possible."

Which shows that the reporter did not know of the existence of their captain's sister.

When I came in, the score was fifty-one for nine, and Henry was still in. I had only one ball to play, so I feel that I should describe it in full. I have four good scoring strokes—the cut, the drive, the hook and the glance. As the bowler ran up to the crease I decided to cut the ball to the ropes. Directly, however, it left his hand, I saw that it was a ball to hook, and accordingly I changed my attitude to the one usually adopted for that stroke. But the ball came up farther than I expected, so at the last moment I drove it hard past the bowler. That at least was the idea. Actually, it turned out to be a beautiful glance shot to the leg boundary. Seldom, if ever, has Beldam had such an opportunity for four action photographs on one plate.

Henry took a sixer next ball, and so we won. And the rest of the story of my team, is it not written in the journals of *The Sportsman* and *The Chartleigh Watchman*, and in the hearts of all who were privileged to compose it? But how the editor took two jokes I told him in the train, and put them in his paper (as his own), and how Carey challenged the engine-driver to an eighteen-hole solitaire match, and how ... these things indeed shall never be divulged.

EX NIHILO FIT MULTUM

I should like to explain just what happened to the ball. In the first place it was of an irreproachable length, and broke very sharply and cleverly from the leg. (The bowler, I am sure, will bear me out in this.) Also it rose with great suddenness ... and, before I had time to perfect any adequate system of defence, took me on the knee, and from there rolled on to the off-stump. There was a considerable amount of applause on the part of the field, due, no doubt, to the feeling that a dangerous batsman had been dismissed without scoring. I need hardly add that I did not resent this appreciation.

What I really wished to say to the wicket-keeper was (1) that it was the first fast wicket I had played on this summer; (2) that it was my first nought this season, and, hang it, even Fry made noughts sometimes; and (3) that personally I always felt that it didn't matter what one made oneself so long as one's side was victorious. What I actually said was shorter; but I expect the wicket-keeper understood just as well. He seemed an intelligent fellow.

After that, I walked nine miles back to the pavilion.

The next man was brushing his hair in the dressing-room.

"What's happened?" he asked.

"Nothing," I said truthfully.

"But you're out, aren't you?"

"I mean that nothing has eventuated — accrued, as it were."

"Blob? Bad luck. Is my parting straight?"

"It curls a bit from leg up at the top, but it will do. Mind you make some. I always feel that so long as one's side is victorious— —"

But he was gone. I brushed my own hair very carefully, lit a cigarette, and went outside to the others. I always think that a nought itself is nothing — the way one carries it off is everything. A disaster, not only to himself but also to his side, should not make a man indifferent to his personal appearance.

"Bad luck," said somebody. "Did it come back?"

"Very quickly. We both did."

"He wasn't breaking much when I was in," said some tactless idiot.

"Then why did you get out?" I retorted.

"L.b.w."

I moved quickly away from him, and sat next to a man who had yet to go in.

"Bad luck," he said. "Second ball, wasn't it? I expect I shall do the same."

I thought for a moment.

"What makes you think you will have a second?" I asked.

"To judge from the easy way in which those two are knocking the bowling about, I sha'n't even have a first," he smiled.

I moved on again.

"Hallo," said a voice. "I saw you get out. How many did you make?"

"None," I said wearily.

"How many?"

I went and sat down next to him.

"Guess," I said.

"Oh, I can't."

"Well, think of a number."

"Yes."

"Double it. Divide by two. Take away the number you first thought of. What does that make?"

"A hundred."

"You must have done it wrong," I said suspiciously.

"No, I am sure I didn't.... No, it still comes to a hundred."

"Well, then, I must have made a hundred," I said excitedly. "Are you *sure* you haven't made a mistake?"

"Quite."

"Then I'd better go and tell the scorer. He put me down a blob—silly ass."

"He's a bad scorer, I know."

"By the way," I said, as I got up, "what number did you think of?"

"Well, it's like this. When you asked me to guess what you had made I instinctively thought of blob, only I didn't like to say so. Then when you began that number game I started with a hundred—it's such an easy number. Double—two hundred. Divided by two—one hundred. Take away the number you first thought of—that's blob, and you have a hundred left. Wasn't that right?"

"You idiot," I said angrily. "Of course it wasn't."

"Well, don't get sick about it. We all make mistakes."

"Sick, I'm not sick. Only just for the moment.... I really thought.... Well, I shall never be so near a century again."

At lunch I sat next to one of their side.

"How many did you make?" he asked.

"Not very many," I said.

"How many?"

"Oh, hardly any. None at all, practically."

"How many actually?"

"*And* actually," I said. ("Fool.") .

After lunch a strange man happened to be talking to me.

"And why did *you* get out?" he asked.

It was a silly question and deserved a silly answer. Besides, I was sick of it all by this time.

"Point's moustache put me off," I said.

"What was wrong with Point's moustache?"

"It swerved the wrong way."

"I was fielding point," he said.

"I'm very sorry. But if you had recognised me, you wouldn't have asked why I got out, and if I had recognised you I shouldn't have told you. So let's forgive and forget."

I hoped that the subject was really closed this time. Of course, I knew that kind friends and relations would ask me on the morrow how many I had made, but for that day I wanted no more of it. Yet, as it happened, I reopened the subject myself.

For with five minutes to play their ninth wicket fell. Mid-off sauntered over towards me.

"Just as well we didn't stay in any longer."

"That's *just* what I thought," I said triumphantly, "all along."

AN AVERAGE MAN

Of Tomkins as a natural cricketer
It frequently has been remarked—that IF
He'd had more opportunities of bowling,
And rather more encouragement in batting,
And IF his averages, so disclosed,
Batting and bowling, had been interchanged;
And IF the field as usually set
Contained some post (at the pavilion end)
Whose presence rather than a pair of hands
Was called for; then, before the season finished,
Tomkins would certainly have played for Kent.

All this, however, is beside the mark.
Just now I wish to hymn the glorious day
(Ignored by those who write the almanacs,
Unnoticed by the calendar compilers),
That Wednesday afternoon, twelve months ago
When Tomkins raised his average to two.

Thanks to an interval of accidents
(As "Tomkins did not bat"—and "not out 0,"
But this more rarely) Tomkins' average
Had long remained at 1.3.
(Though Tomkins, sacrificing truth to pride,
Or both to euphony, left out the dot—

Left out the little dot upon the three,
Only employing it to justify
A second three to follow on the first.
Thus, if a stranger asked his average
Tomkins would answer "One point thirty-three"—
Nor lay the stress unduly on the "one" ...).

A curious thing is custom! There are men—
Plum Warner is, of course, a case in point—
Who cannot bat unless they go in first.

Others, as Hayes and Denton, have their place
First wicket down; while Number Six or so
Is suited best to Jessop. As for Tomkins
His place was always one above the Byes,
And three above the Wides. So Custom willed.

Upon this famous Wednesday afternoon
Wickets had fallen fast before the onslaught
Of one who had, as Euclid might have put it,
No length, or break, but only pace; and pace
Had been too much for nine of them already.
Then entered Tomkins the invincible.
Took guard as usual, "just outside the leg,"
Looked round the field, and mentally decided
To die—or raise his average to two.
Whereon—for now the bowler was approaching,
He struck a scientific attitude,
Advanced the left leg firmly down the pitch,
And swung his bat along the line AB
(See Ranjitsinhji's famous book of cricket).

And when the bat and leg were both at B
(Having arrived there more or less together),
Then Tomkins, with his usual self-effacement,
Modestly closed his eyes, and left the rest
To Providence and Ranjy and the bowler
(Forming a quorum); two at least of whom
Resolved that he should neatly glide the ball
Somewhere between the first and second slips.
So Tomkins did compile a chanceless two.

Once more the bowler rushed upon the crease,
While Tomkins made a hasty calculation
(Necessitating use of decimals)
And found his average was 1.5.
So lustily he smote and drove the ball
Loftily over long stop's head for one;
Which brought the decimal to seventy-five,
And Tomkins, puffing, to the other end.

Then, feeling that the time for risks was come,
He rolled his sleeves up, blew upon his hands,
And played back to a yorker, and was bowled.

Every position has its special charm.
You go in first and find as a reward
The wicket at its best; you go in later
And find the fielders slack, the bowling loose.
Tomkins, who went in just above the Byes,
Found one of them had slipped into his score.
'Tis wise to take the good the gods provide you—
And Tomkins has an average of two.

SMALL GAMES

PHYSICAL CULTURE

"Why don't you sit up?" said Adela at dinner, suddenly prodding me in the back. Adela is old enough to take a motherly interest in my figure, and young enough to look extremely pretty while doing so.

"I always stoop at meals," I explained; "it helps the circulation. My own idea."

"But it looks so bad. You ought — — "

"Don't improve me," I begged,

"No wonder you have — — "

"Hush! I haven't. I got a bullet on the liver in the campaign of '03, due to over-smoking, and sometimes it hurts me a little in the cold weather. That's all."

"Why don't you try the Hyperion?"

"I will. Where is it?"

"It isn't anywhere; you buy it."

"Oh, I thought you dined at it. What do you buy it for?"

"It's one of those developers with elastics and pulleys and so on. Every morning early, for half-an-hour before breakfast — — "

"You *are* trying to improve me," I said suspiciously.

"But they are such good things," went on Adela earnestly. "They really do help to make you beautiful — — "

"I *am* beautiful."

"Well, much more beautiful. And strong — — "

"Are you being simply as tactful as you can be?"

" — and graceful."

"It isn't as though you were actually a relation," I protested.

Adela continued, full of her ideas:

"It would do you so much good, you know. Would you promise me to use it every day if I sent you mine?"

"Why don't you want yours any more now? Are you perfect now?"

"You can easily hook it to the wall——"

"I suppose," I reflected, "there is a limit of beauty beyond which it is dangerous to go. After that, either the thing would come off the hook, or——"

"Well," said Adela suddenly, "aren't I looking well?"

"You're looking radiant," I said appreciatively; "but it may only be because you're going to marry Billy next month."

She smiled and blushed. "Well, I'll send it to you," she said. "And you try it for a week, and then tell me if you don't feel better. Oh, and don't do all the exercises to begin with; start with three or four of the easy ones."

"Of course," I said.

I undid the wrappings eagerly, took off the lid of the box, and was confronted with (apparently) six pairs of braces. I shook them out of the box and saw I had made a mistake. It was one pair of braces for Magog. I picked it up, and I knew that I was in the presence of the Hyperion. In five minutes I had screwed a hook into the bedroom wall and attached the beautifier. Then I sat on the edge of the bed and looked at it.

There was a tin plate, fastened to the top, with the word "LADIES" on it. I got up, removed it with a knife, and sat down again. Everything was very dusty, and I wondered when Adela had last developed herself.

By-and-by I went into the other room to see if I had overlooked anything. I found on the floor a chart of exercises, and returned triumphantly with it.

There were thirty exercises altogether, and the chart gave

(1) A detailed explanation of how to do each particular exercise;

(2) A photograph of a lady doing it.

"After all," I reassured myself, after the first bashful glance, "it is Adela who has thrust this upon me; and she must have known." So I studied it.

Nos. 10, 15 and 28 seemed the easiest; I decided to confine myself to them. For the first of these you strap yourself in at the waist, grasp the handles, and fall slowly backwards until your head touches the floor—all the elastic cords being then at full stretch. When I had got very slowly halfway down, an extra piece of elastic which had got hitched somewhere came suddenly into play, and I did the rest of the journey without a stop, finishing up sharply against the towel horse. The chart had said, "Inhale going down," and I was inhaling hard at the moment that the towel horse and two damp towels spread themselves over my face.

"So much for Exercise 10," I thought, as I got up. "I'll just get the idea to-night, and then start properly to-morrow. Now for No. 15."

Somehow I felt instinctively that No. 15 would cause trouble. For No. 15 you stand on the right foot, fasten the left foot to one of the cords, and stretch it out as far as you can....

What—officially—you do then, I cannot say....

Some people can stand easily upon the right foot, when the left is fastened to the wall ... others cannot ... it is a gift....

Having recovered from my spontaneous rendering of No. 15 I turned to No. 28. This one, I realised, was extremely important; I would do it twelve times.

You begin by lying flat on the floor, roped in at the waist, and with your hands (grasping the elastic cords) held straight up in the air. The tension on your waist is then extreme, but on your hands only moderate. Then, taking a deep breath, you pull your arms slowly out until they lie along the floor. The tension becomes terrific, the strain on every part of you is immense. While I lay there, taking a deep breath before relaxing, I said to myself, "The strain will be too much for me."

I was wrong. It was too much for the hook. The hook whizzed out, everything flew at me at once, and I remembered no more....

As I limped into bed, I trod heavily upon something sharp. I shrieked and bent down to see what had bitten me. It was a tin plate bearing the words "LADIES."

"Well?" said Adela, a week later.

I looked at her for a long time.

"When did you last use the Hyperion?" I asked.

"About a year ago."

"Ah! ... You don't remember the chart that went with it?"

"Not well. Except, of course, that each exercise was arranged for a particular object according to what you wanted."

"Exactly. So I discovered yesterday. It was in very small type, and I missed it at first."

"Well, how many did you do?"

"I limited myself to Exercises 10, 15, and 28. Do you happen to remember what those were for?"

"Not particularly."

"No. Well, I started with No. 10. No. 10, you may recall, is one of the most perilous. I nearly died over No. 10. And when I had been doing it for a week, I discovered what its particular object was."

"What?"

"'*To round the forearm!*' Yes, madam," I said bitterly, "I have spent a week of agony ... and I have rounded one forearm."

"Why didn't you try another?"

"I did. I tried No. 15. Six times in the pursuit of No. 15 have I been shot up to the ceiling by the left foot ... and what for, Adela? '*To arch the instep!*' Look at my instep! Why should I want to arch it?"

"I wish I could remember which chart I sent you," said Adela, wrinkling her brow.

"It was the wrong one," I said....

There was a long silence.

"Oh," said Adela suddenly, "you never told me about No. 28."

"Pardon me," I said, "I cannot bear to speak of 28."

"Why, was it even more unsuitable than the other two?"

"I found, when I had done it six times, that its object was stated to be, '*To remove double chin.*' That, however, was not the real effect. And so I crossed out the false comment and wrote the true one in its place."

"And what is that?" asked Adela.

"'*To remove the hook,*'" I said gloomily.

CROQUET

PROLOGUE

"I hear you're very good at croquet," said my hostess.

"Oh, well," I said modestly. (The fact is I can beat them all at home.)

"We have the North Rutland champion staying with us. He's very keen on a game. Now then, how can we manage?"

This was terrible. I must put it off somehow.

"*Is* there a north to Rutland," I began argumentatively. "I always thought——"

"Yes, I see. He shall play with Jane against you and Miss Middleton. By the way, let me introduce you all."

We bowed to each other for a bit, and then I had another shock. The N.R. champion's mallet was bound with brass at each end (in case he wanted to hit backwards suddenly) and had a silver plate on it. Jane's had the brass only. It was absurd that they should play together.

I drew Miss Middleton on one side.

"I say," I began nervously, "I'm frightfully sorry, but I quite forgot to bring my mallet. Will it matter very much?"

"I haven't one either."

"You know, when my man was packing my bag, I particularly said to him, 'Now, don't forget to put in a mallet.' He said, 'Shall I put the spare one in too, sir, because the best one's sprung a bit?'"

"Oh, I've never had one of my own. I suppose when one is really good——"

"Well, to tell you the truth, I've never had one either. We're fairly in for it now."

"Never mind, we'll amuse ourselves somehow, I expect."

"Oh, I'm quite looking forward to it."

CHAPTER I

They kicked off from the summer-house end, and, after jockeying for the start a bit, the N.R. champion got going. He went very slowly but very surely. I watched anxiously for ten minutes, expecting my turn every moment. After a quarter of an hour I raised my hat and moved away.

"Shall we sit down?" I said to Miss Middleton.

"We shall be in the way if we sit down here, sha'n't we?"

"Outside that chalk line we're safe?"

"I—I suppose so."

We moved outside and sat down on the grass.

"I never even had a chalk line," I said mournfully.

"It's much more fun without."

"You know," I went on, "I can beat them all at home. Why even Wilfrid——"

"It's just the same with me," said Miss Middleton. "Hilda did win once by a frightful fluke, but——"

"But this is quite different. At home it would be considered jolly bad form to go on all this time."

"One would simply go in and leave them," said Miss Middleton.

"You know, it's awful fun at home. The lawn goes down in terraces, and if you hit the other person's ball hard enough you can get it right down to the bottom; and it takes at least six to get back on the green again."

Miss Middleton gurgled to herself.

"We've got a stream ... round our lawn," she said, in gasps. "It's such a joke ... and once ... when Hilda..."

CHAPTER II

"May I call you 'Mary?'" I said; "we're still here."

"Well, we have known each other a long time, certainly," said Miss Middleton. "I think you might."

"Thanks very much."

"What hoop is he at?"

"He's just half-way."

"I suppose, when he's finished, then, Jane does it all?"

"It practically comes to that. I believe, as a matter of form, I am allowed a shot in between."

"That won't make any difference, will it?"

"No...."

"It's awfully hot, isn't it?"

"Yes.... Do you bicycle much?"

"No.... Do you?"

"No. I generally sleep in the afternoons."

"Much the best thing to do. Good-night."

"Good-night."

CHAPTER III

"Wake up," I said. "You've been asleep for hours. Jane is playing now."

"Oh, I'm so sorry," said Mary, still with her eyes closed. "Then I missed your turn. Was it a good one?"

"Absolutely splendid. I had a very long shot, and hit the champion. Then I took my mallet in both hands, brought it well over the shoulder—are you allowed to do that, by the way?"

"Yes, it's hockey where you mustn't."

"And croqueted him right down to the house—over beds, through bushes, across paths—the longest ball I've ever driven."

"I hope you didn't make him very cross. You see, he may not be used to our game."

"Cross? My dear girl, he was fairly chuckling with delight. Told me I'd missed the rest of my turn. It seems that if you go over two beds, and across more than one path, you miss the rest of your turn. Did you know that?"

"I suppose I did really, but I'd forgotten."

"And here I am again. Jane will be even longer. He's lying on the grass, and taking sights for her just now.... Why didn't you answer my last letter?"

CHAPTER IV

"It's this passion for games," I said, waking up suddenly, "which has made us Englishmen what we are. Here we have a hot July afternoon, when all Nature is at peace, and the foreigner is taking his siesta. And what do we do? How do we English men and women spend this hot afternoon? Why, immediately after lunch, in one case even before the meal has been digested, we rush off to take part in some violent game like croquet. Hour after hour the play goes on relentlessly; there is no backing out on our part, no pleading for just five minutes in which to get our wind. No, we bear our part manfully, and — — Are you awake by any chance, or am I wasting all this?"

"Of course I'm awake," said Mary, opening her eyes.

"What years I have known you! Do you remember those days when we used to paddle together—the mixed paddling at Brighton?"

"Ah, yes. And your first paint-box."

"And your doll — —"

"And the pony — —"

"And the—good-night."

"G'night."

CHAPTER XVIII

"But how absurd," said Mary, "when we've only just met."

"Oh, but come; it was about two years ago that you let me call you 'Mary.'"

"True," said Mary thoughtfully.

"And you can't say we aren't suited to one another. We both play without the chalk line."

"So we do. Yet ... Oh, I can't say all at once. Give me a little time."

"I'll give you three of Jane's hoops. That's about six months."

CHAPTER XX

"Twenty-eight," said the North Rutland champion. "That's what I won the championship by, I remember."

"It's a good winning score," I said. "Do they play much in North Rutland?"

"I'm afraid it's been very slow for you and Miss Middleton," said Jane.

"Not exactly slow," I said.

"We've been talking a lot of nonsense," explained Miss Middleton.

"Not exactly nonsense," said I.

"Oh, it was," said Miss Middleton, "you know it was."

"I suppose it was," I sighed. "Well, we'll try again to-morrow."

"Right," said the champion. "But I shall use my other mallet."

GARDENING

There may be gardeners who can appear to be busy all the year round — doing even in the winter their little bit under glass. But for myself I wait reverently until the twenty-second of March is here. Then, spring having officially arrived, I step out on to the lawn, and summon my head-gardener.

"James," I say, "the winter is over at last. What have we got in that big brown-looking bed in the middle there?"

"Well, sir," he says, "we don't seem to have anything, do we, like?"

"Perhaps there's something down below that hasn't pushed through yet?"

"Maybe there is."

"I wish you knew more about it," I say angrily; "I want to bed out the macaroni there. Have we got a spare bed, with nothing going on underneath?"

"I don't know, sir. Shall I dig 'em up and have a look?"

"Yes, perhaps you'd better," I say.

Between ourselves, James is a man of no initiative. He has to be told everything.

However, mention of him brings me to my first rule for young gardeners —

Never sow Spring Onions and New Potatoes in the
same bed

I did this by accident last year. The fact is, when the onions were given to me I quite thought they were young daffodils; a mistake anyone might make. Of course, I don't generally keep daffodils and potatoes together; but James swore that the hard round things were tulip bulbs. It is perfectly useless to pay your head-gardener half-a-crown a week if he doesn't know the difference between potatoes and tulip bulbs. Well, anyhow, there they were in the herbaceous border together, and they grew up side by side; the onions getting stronger every day and the potatoes more sensitive. At last, just when they were ripe for picking, I found that the young onions had actually brought tears to the eyes of the potatoes—to such an extent that the latter were too damp for baking or roasting, and had to be mashed. Now, as everybody knows, mashed potatoes are beastly.

THE RHUBARB BORDER

gives me more trouble than all the rest of the garden. I started it a year ago with the idea of keeping the sun off the young carnations. It acted excellently, and the complexion of the flowers was improved tenfold. Then one day I discovered James busily engaged in pulling up the rhubarb.

"What are you doing?" I cried. "Do you want the young carnations to go all brown?"

"I was going to send some in to the cook," he grumbled.

"To the cook! What do you mean? Rhubarb isn't a vegetable."

"No, it's a fruit."

I looked at James anxiously. He had a large hat on, and the sun couldn't have got to the back of his neck.

"My dear James," I said, "I don't pay you half-a-crown a week for being funny. Perhaps we had better make it two shillings in future."

However, he persisted in his theory that in the spring people stewed rhubarb in tarts and ate it!

Well, I have discovered since that this is actually so. People really do grow it in their gardens, not with the idea of keeping the sun off the young carnations but under the impression that it is a fruit. Consequently, I have found it necessary to adopt a firm line with my friends' rhubarb. On arriving at any house for a visit, the first thing I say to my host is, "May I see your rhubarb bed? I have heard such a lot about it."

"By all means," he says, feeling rather flattered, and leads the way into the garden.

"What a glorious sunset," I say, pointing to the west.

"Isn't it," he says, turning round; and then I surreptitiously drop a pint of weed-killer on the bed.

Next morning I get up early and paint the roots of the survivors with iodine.

Once my host, who for some reason had got up early too, discovered me.

"What are you doing?" he asked.

"Just painting the roots with iodine," I said, "to prevent the rhubarb falling out."

"To prevent what?"

"To keep the green fly away," I corrected myself. "It's the new French intensive system."

But he was suspicious, and I had to leave two or three stalks untreated. We had those for lunch that day. There was only one thing for a self-respecting man to do. I obtained a large plateful of the weed and emptied the sugar basin and the cream jug over it. Then I took a mouthful of the pastry, gave a little start, and said, "Oh, is this rhubarb? I'm sorry, I didn't know." Whereupon I pushed my plate away and started on the cheese.

ASPARAGUS

Asparagus wants watching very carefully. It requires to be tended like a child. Frequently, I wake up in the middle of the night and wonder if James has remembered to put the hot-water bottle in the asparagus bed. Whenever I get up to look I find that he has forgotten.

He tells me to-day that he is beginning to think that the things which are coming up now are not asparagus after all, but young hyacinths. This is very annoying. I am inclined to fancy that James is not the man he was. For the sake of his reputation in the past I hope he is not.

POTTING OUT

I have spent a busy morning potting out the nasturtiums. We have them in three qualities—mild, medium and full. Nasturtiums are extremely peppery flowers, and take offence so quickly that the utmost tact is required to pot them successfully. In a general way all the red or reddish flowers should be potted as soon as they are old enough to stand it, but it is considered bad form among horticulturists to pot the white.

James has been sowing the roses. I wanted all the pink ones in one bed, and all the yellow ones in another, and so on; but James says you never can tell for certain what colour a flower is going to be until it comes up. Of course, any fool could tell then.

"You should go by the picture on the outside of the packet," I said.

"They're very misleading," said James.

"Anyhow, they must be all brothers in the same packet."

"You might have a brother with red hair," says James.

I hadn't thought of that.

GRAFTING

Grafting is when you try short approaches over the pergola in somebody's else's garden, and break the best tulip. You mend it with a ha'penny stamp and hope that nobody will notice; at any rate not until you have gone away on the Monday. Of course in your own garden you never want to graft.

I hope at some future time to be allowed—even encouraged—to refer to such things as the most artistic way to frame cucumbers, how to stop tomatoes blushing (the hom[oe]opathic method of putting them next to the French beans is now discredited), and spring fashions in fox gloves. But for the moment I have said enough. The great thing to remember in gardening is that flowers, fruits and vegetables alike can only be cultivated with sympathy. Special attention should be given to backward and delicate plants. They should be encouraged to make the most of themselves. Never forget that flowers, like ourselves, are particular about the company they keep. If a hyacinth droops in the celery bed, put it among the pansies.

But above all, mind, a firm hand with the rhubarb.

GOLF

CHAPTER I

The documents in the case are these:

Him to Me

"Come and play golf on Thursday. What is your handicap? I expect you will be too good for me."

Me to Him

"MY GOOD THOMAS,—Don't be silly. I will play you at cricket, tennis, lawn tennis, football (both codes), croquet, poker-patience, high diving and here-we-go-round-the-mulberry-bush. If you insist, I will take you on at prisoners' base and billiards. Moreover I can dance the *pavane*. Yours ever,

"ADOLPHUS

"*P.S.*—Anyhow, I haven't any clubs."

Him to Me

"MY DEAR ASS,—I gather that you aren't a golfer; well, why not begin on Thursday? There will be nobody else playing probably. Meet me at Victoria eleven-five. My brother is away, and I will lend you his clubs."

Me to Him

(Telegram)

"Is your brother out of England? Wire reply."

Him to Me

"Yes. Sicily."

Me to Him

"Right you are then."

CHAPTER II

"You know," I said to Thomas in the train, "I have played a little on a very small island off the coast of Scotland, but it was such a very small island that we never used a driver at all, or—what's that other thing called?—a brassy. We should have been into the sea in no time. But I rather fancy myself with a putter."

"You might go round with a putter to-day."

"I might, but I sha'n't. I expect to use the wooden clubs with great ease and dexterity. And I think you will find that I can do some business with the mashie. What's a niblick?"

"The thing you get out of bunkers with."

"Then I sha'n't want that."

CHAPTER III

The fateful moment arrived. Thomas presented me with a ball called the Colonel, and a caddie offered me Thomas's brother's driver. He also asked me what sort of tee I should like.

I leant upon my club and looked at him. Then I turned to Thomas.

"Our young friend Hector," I said, "is becoming technical. Will you explain?"

"Well, do you want a high or a low one?"

"I want to hit this Colonel ball very hard in the direction of that flag. What do you recommend?"

"Well, that's just as you——"

"I think a medium one. Slow to medium."

The preliminaries being arranged, I proceeded to address the ball. My own instinct was to take the address as read and get to business as soon as possible, but in the presence of an expert like Hector I did not dare to omit the trimmings. As it was, after every waggle I felt less and less like hitting the Colonel. When at last I did let fly it was with feelings of relief that I discovered, on returning an eye to the spot, that the tee was indeed empty. I shaded my eyes and gazed into the middle distance.

"No," said Thomas, "it's more to the right." He indicated a spot in the foreground, about ten yards E.N.E. "There you are."

"That isn't *my* ball."

"Yes, sir," said Hector, grinning.

"May I have it back?"

Thomas laughed and smote his own into the blue. "You go on from there," he said.

"I'm still aiming at the same flag?"

"Go on, you ass."

I went on. The ball again rolled ten yards to the east.

"I don't know why we're going in this direction," I said. "If I get much further east I shall have to send back Bartlett. You know, I don't believe the Colonel is taking this seriously. He doesn't seem to me to be trying at all. Has he ever been round the course before?"

"Never. He's quite new to it."

"There you are. He'll come down at the ditch for a certainty."

I played my third. A third time we went ten yards to the east—well, perhaps with a touch of north in it again. And this time Hector gave a sudden snort of laughter.

I leant upon my club, and stared him into gravity. Then I took Thomas by the coat and led him on one side.

"There are, Thomas," I said, "other things than golf."

"There are," he agreed.

"A man may fail temporarily at the game and yet not be wholly despicable."

"True."

"He may, for instance, be able to dance the *pavane* with grace and distinction."

"Quite so."

"Well then, *will* you take this giggling child away and explain to him that I am not such an ass as I appear? Tell him that the intellectuals of Brook Green think highly of my mental powers. Assure him that in many of the best houses at Wandsworth Common I am held to be an amusing raconteur. Remind him of my *villanelle* 'To Autumn.' For heaven's sake make him understand that my reputation does not stand or fall with my ability to use this brassy thing. I'm not a golf professional."

Thomas allowed himself to smile. "I will tell him," he said, "that you are not a golf professional."

We veered right round to the east with my fourth and then I became desperate.

"Why," I shouted, "do I hit the ball with a ridiculous club like this? I could send it farther with a cricket bat. I could push it straighter with a billiard cue. Where's that bag? I am going to have a lucky dip."

I dipped, and came up with what Thomas called a cleek. "Now then," I said. I didn't stop to address the Colonel, I simply lashed at him. He flew along the ground at a terrific pace.

"Well kept down," said Thomas admiringly.

"By Jove!" I cried, "that's never going to stop. See how he flies along ... now he breasts the slope ... look, he is taking the water jump.... Ah, he has crossed his legs, he's down."

"This," I said to Thomas as we walked after the Colonel, "is golf. A glorious game."

"What nonsense," I said to Thomas, "they put in comic papers about golf. All that about digging up the turf! ... and missing the ball! ... and breaking the clubs! I mean, I simply don't see how one *could*! Let's see, I've played four, haven't I?"

"Five," said Thomas. "What I am wondering," he added, "is why you should have been afraid of using any club in your small island off the coast of Scotland."

CHAPTER IV

Twenty Strokes After

"The green, the green," I shouted joyfully, in the manner of the ancient Greeks, though I was only on the edge of it.

"Go on," said Thomas.

I took a careful aim and put the white down.

"You see," I said carelessly, leaning on my putter.

STUMP CRICKET

April will soon be here," said Miss Middleton, with a sigh of happiness.

"Bless it," I agreed. "My favourite month. Twelve," I added conversationally, "is my lucky number, and Thursday the day of the week on which I do least work. When next the twelfth of April falls on a Thursday, which may not be for centuries, look out. Something terrific will happen."

"It's about now that one begins to wonder if one is in form, or likely to be."

"Just about now," I agreed. "I always say that when the draw is announced for the semi-finals of the English Cup, in which, of course, I take not the slightest interest whatever, and in fact hardly know what teams are left in for it, though I must say I hope Southampton wins this year, because, after all, Fry did play for them once, but they'll have a bit of a job to beat the Wolves you know—and then there's Newcastle and Fulham after that, and of course, you can't be ..."

"I'm tired of that sentence," said Miss Middleton.

"So was I. I only wanted to make it clear that I have no use for these spectacular gladiatorial combats. Give me cricket, the game of——"

Miss Middleton did not appear to be listening.

"Do you bowl as fast and as good a length as you talk?" she asked thoughtfully.

"No. More swerve perhaps. And I bowl with my head a good deal."

"I see. Quite different. Well, then, will you coach me this spring? Do, there's a dear."

"I should love to. I know all the things to say."

She got up excitedly.

"Come along then. I've got the rippingest bat. But you must promise not to bowl too fast."

I had said that I knew all the things to say, but as a matter of fact there is only one thing to say: "You should have come out to 'er, sir." (Or, I suppose, in Miss Middleton's case, "You should have come out to him, madam.") It's a silly remark to make, because it is just what one is always doing. At school I could come out to anything that was straight and not too high; the difficulty lay in staying in. Nobody ever told me how to do that.

Miss Middleton led the way to a walled-in tennis lawn, which lay next to the broccoli tops and things, and was kept away from it by only six feet of brick. If it had simply been a question of cabbage I should have said nothing, but there would be grapes there too.

"I know," said Miss Middleton. "But we must play against a wall. Don't bowl too much to leg."

I hadn't bowled since October the Fourth. The first post-October ball was a trifle over-pitched, and a little too much to the right. All the same I was just saying, "You should have come out to that one," when there was a crash from the direction of long-on.

"By Jove, I didn't know you were so good. Was that the grapes?"

"How awful! Yes. It simply seemed to fly off the bat. I did ask you not to bowl there, didn't I?"

She looked so penitent that I had to comfort her.

"It's all right," I said consolingly. "I had a man there. You would have been out all the way. Besides," I went on, "a little air will do the grapes good. They stay all the time in one hot room, and then when they go out into the cold, they don't muffle up, and the natural consequence is — — Or am I thinking of influenza?"

"Never mind. We must remember not to do it again, that's all. Give me some to cut."

There are several ways of cutting. For myself, I was taught to cut "square" with the left leg across and "late" with the right, the consequence being that I can do neither. W.G. (to work downwards) generally uses the fore-arm for the stroke, Ranji the wrist. Miss Middleton keeps both feet together and puts her whole body into it; and the direction in which the ball travels is towards long-on. There was another crash.

"Golf is your game," I said admiringly. "You lay it dead on the greenhouse every time."

"I say, what *shall* we do? Father will be furious."

I looked at my watch.

"I can just catch the three-twenty-five," I said.

"Oh, don't be a coward, when it's all your fault for bowling so badly."

"Perhaps the glass is insured," I suggested. "It is generally."

"It's insured against hail," she said doubtfully.

I looked at the sky. It was one of the most beautiful blues I have seen.

"No," said Miss Middleton sadly.

"It will be a point for lawyers to argue, I fancy, what is actually meant by hail. You would probably define it at once as aqueous vapour cooled down in the atmosphere to the freezing point of water."

"I don't know. Perhaps I should."

"But 'hail' here obviously has a wider significance. I take it to mean 'anything that descends suddenly from the clouds.' I haven't 'Williams on Real Property' with me, but— —"

"Come on," said Miss Middleton, "let's say it does mean that. And could you, *please*, keep them a bit more on the off?"

"It's no good my keeping them there if you don't."

The worst of coaching—I speak now as an expert—is that it is so difficult to know what to say when a lady whirls her bat twice round her head, gives a little shriek, gets the ball on the knee, and says, "What ought I to have done then?" The only answer I could think of was "Not that."

"I thought you knew all about coaching," she said scornfully.

"But, you see, it depends on what you were wanting to do," I said meekly. "If it was a drive you should have come out to it more, and if it was a cut you should have come down on it; while if it was a Highland fling you lacked *abandon*, and if you were killing a wasp— —"

"A good coach would know what was the best thing to do with that particular ball, wouldn't he? And that's just what he would tell you."

"He wouldn't know," I said modestly. "You don't often meet that sort of ball in good cricket."

"No, I suppose not. That's why I didn't know what to do, I expect. You know I generally know exactly what to do, only I can't do it."

"Is that really so?" I cried excitedly. "Why, then, of course, you ought to coach *me*!"

We had a very jolly afternoon. I fancy I shall be in some form this year. Miss Middleton is one of the best bowlers I have seen, but I brought off some beautiful shots. I wanted some tea badly afterwards.

"What glorious days we have now," said Miss Middleton's mother, as she handed me a cup.

"Glorious," said Miss Middleton's father.

"H'm, yes," I said doubtfully. "But you know I'm afraid it won't last. It's beginning to look rather like—like hail."

"Yes," said Miss Middleton. "We both thought so."

EXPLORING

Come, gather around, my 'earties, and listen
    a while to me,
For I 'ave a yarn to spin you, a yarn of the
    Polar Sea;
It's as true as I'm standing here, lads, as true as it
    blows a gale,
That I was the first as nearly burst a-finding the
    Great Big Nail—
As sworn to by Etukishook, Gaukrodger, J. C. Clegg,
    Sir Fortescue Flannery, and the Cardinal
    Merry del Val.

It was all of a parky morning that wunnerful fourth
    of March,
When I put on a hextry weskit and made for the
    Marble Arch;
So I sez good-bye to my country, "Lunnon," I sez,
    "adoo!"
And I up and strode down the Edgware Road
    athirsting to see it through,
Followed by Etukishook, Gaukrodger, J. C. Clegg,
    Sir Fortescue Flannery, and the Cardinal
    Merry del Val.

I 'adn't no blooming gum-drops, I 'adn't no polar
    bears,
I 'adn't no sextant neither, but I thinks to myself,
    "'Oo cares?"
And I waggled my watch-chain jaunty, which was
    jewelled in every hole.
"I can always steer by my cumpas 'ere, it's pointing
    straight to the Pole."
So it is!" said Etukishook, Gaukrodger, J. C. Clegg,
    Sir Fortescue Flannery, and the Cardinal
    Merry del Val.

I walked for the 'ole of that morning, then I sez
    to myself, "Old son,
This here is a dash-for-the-Pole like, and it's
    darn little dash you've done."
So I enters an 'andy station, and I sez to the
    man in the 'utch,
"'Ere, gimme a ticket as goes to Wick—no, a
    first-return—'ow much?—
Ah, and five third singles for Etukishook, Gaukrodger,
    J. C. Clegg, Sir Fortescue Flannery, and the
    Cardinal Merry del Val."

We sailed from Wick to the norrard for 'undreds
    of days and nights.
Till we came at last to the ice-floes and followed the
    Northern Lights,
The Horroreo-boreo-balis, which it turned us all
    'orrible pale,
And I sez to my men, "To-morrow and then we
    shall land at the Great Big Nail."
"'Ooray!" said Etukishook, Gaukrodger, J. C. Clegg,
    Sir Fortescue Flannery and the Cardinal Merry
    del Val.

'Twas the cumpas as went and found it—it seemed
    to have turned its head,
It would spin like mad for a minute and then it
    would lay like dead;
It took on just like a wild thing, you'd almost 'a'
    sworn it cried,
Till at last it shot through the glass and got right up
    on its end and died.
"That *proves* it," cried Etukishook, Gaukrodger,
    J. C. Clegg, Sir Fortescue Flannery, and the
    Cardinal Merry del Val.

We gave three cheers for ole England and we up
    with the Union Jack,
And we plugged our pipes and we smoked
    'em and we thought about getting back;
But a wunnerful pride so filled us as we sat on top
    of the Ball,
That innocent tears (the first for years) rolled out

of the eyes of all.
Partikerlarly out of those of Etukishook, Gaukrodger,
J. C. Clegg, Sir Fortescue Flannery, and the
Cardinal Merry del Val.

Then I called for a pen and paper, and I wrote to
the King, "Dear King,
"I've found the Pole, and I'm tying a piece of it up
with string;
I'll send it round in the morning for your Majesty's
grace to see
Just drop me a wire, if you like it, sire, and I'll
collar the lot! *Signed*: Me.
Witnesses: Etukishook, Gaukrodger, J. C. Clegg, Sir
Fortescue Flannery and the Cardinal Merry
del Val."

So that's how it 'appened, my 'earties, no matter
what others may say.
(Did they *see* the Pole? They didn't! That
proves I 'ad took it away).
It's as true as I'm standing here, lads, as true as
The Daily Mail,
That I was the first as nearly burst a-finding the
Great Big Nail.

SHOPPING

"If you *should* happen to be in Regent Street tomorrow at four" (ran the assignation), "just where what's the name of the street comes into it, and a lady in a very pretty new mauve coat and skirt bows to you, raise your hat and say 'Crisis' and she will let you help her with her shopping."

My guess at the name of the street was successful. I raised my hat and said "Good-afternoon."

"But you had to say 'Crisis,'" said Miss Middleton. "That's the password."

"I can't. I've sworn I'll never say it again. I took a most fearful oath. Several people heard me taking it, and swooned."

"But how do I know you're the right one if you don't say it? Well, I suppose I shall have to let you come. I've just lost mother; she went in at the silver department and out at the art fabrics—like people when they can't pay for their hansoms."

"Yes, that's bad. 'The accused, who appeared to feel her position acutely, gave a false address.' What are you going to buy?"

"Well, I thought I'd just help you get *your* presents first."

"I'm not giving any this Christmas. I gave a lot only a year ago."

"Oh, but haven't they paid you any wages since then?"

"Yes, a few trifling sums, only— — Quick, there's your mother!" I pulled Miss Middleton hastily into the nearest shop and shut the door.

"What fun!" she said breathlessly. "Mother *loves* hide-and-seek."

Mrs Middleton hurried past, covered with parcels, and dived into another door.

"It's quite safe now," I said. "Let's go and— —"

"What can I have the pleasure of showing you?" said a soothing voice at our backs.

We turned round in alarm.

"Er—we only just—let me see, *what* was it you wanted?" said Miss Middleton to me.

"I don't really want anything. I was going to help you buy one of those—you know."

"Yes, but I've got that. I know there was *something* you said you wanted very much."

"Probably tea."

"Tiaras," explained Miss Middleton hastily. "Of course."

"Certainly, madam," said the shopwalker. "If you will just sit down," he continued, leading us to a little room out of the main stream of shoppers, "I will send somebody to attend you."

We sat down mechanically. I leant my stick against a showcase and balanced my hat on the top of it.

"Now you've done it," I said. "How many tiaras shall we have? I've got nearly four pounds."

"We needn't have any. We can say we don't much care about their selection."

"Or that we wanted one specially built for us."

"One goes into dozens of shops without buying *anything*," said Miss Middleton cheerily.

"I never do," I replied gloomily. "Look out, here he is."

An attendant advanced briskly towards us. I put my hands in my pockets and tried to count my money.

"Tiaras, madam? Certainly. About what price?"

"Tell him about three pounds eight and six," I whispered to Miss Middleton. "Three pounds nine," I corrected, as I ran another sixpence to ground.

"Here is a beautiful one at two hundred and fifty pounds."

"Too much," I prompted softly.

"Oh," broke in Miss Middleton brightly, "I'm so sorry—such a silly mistake! We wanted neck-chains, not tiaras! Barbara has a tiara already, hasn't she?" she appealed to me.

"Two," I said quickly. "If not three."

"I'm so sorry," said Miss Middleton, with a dazzling smile. "The first gentleman must have misunderstood. Of course we gave her a tiara last year."

The man was disappointed; I saw that. But the smile melted him, and he went off in all friendliness.

"Tiara doesn't sound very much like neck-chain," I remarked after a pause.

"Oh, don't you think so? It depends how you say it. Like Beauchamp and Cholmondeley."

"And what is it when pronounced properly?"

"It's a chain that hangs round your neck, and when you don't quite know what to say to anybody you play with it carelessly. Same as men smoking cigarettes, only better for you."

"I see. Well, here we have a hundred of the best."

The attendant got to business at once.

"This one," he said, holding up rather a jolly one, "comes out at ten guineas."

"Tell him," I whispered to Miss Middleton, "that we've only come out with three."

"That's *very* pretty," she said. "Are those moon-stones?"

"Yes, madam. The fashionable stone this year."

"It's more for next year that we want it."

"I should say this season. I don't think you will find a prettier one than this, madam."

"It's very sweet. But aren't they unlucky, unless you happen to have been born in the right month?" She turned to me. "When is Barbara's birthday?"

"May," I said unhesitatingly. "I mean March."

"Anyhow," said Miss Middleton. "I know it's wrong for moonstones, because I was thinking of giving her some two years ago, and it had to "be opals instead."

"We both thought of it," I said.

Miss Middleton looked at me so admiringly that I began to get reckless.

"Besides, we don't know the size of her neck," I went on. "And she never smokes—I mean she never doesn't know what to say to anybody. So I think we should be making a mistake if we gave her this. I do indeed. Now if it had been anybody else but Barbara— —"

The man looked from one to the other of us in bewilderment.

"If you could show us some hatpins instead?" said Miss Middleton hurriedly, before he could open his mouth.

"This is excellent," I said, as he retired in confusion; "we're working down well. All we've got to do now is to wait till he comes back and then say that we're sorry but we meant hairpins. With hair-pins you're practically there."

"Supposing they only had gold ones?"

"Then we should point out that they wouldn't go with Barbara's curiously-coloured hair. You leave this to me. I can finish it off now on my head. At the same time I'm sorry I'm not going to spend *anything*."

"Oh, but you are," said Miss Middleton. "You're going to give me and mother tea."

"Of course I am," I agreed.

After tea I went back to the shop by myself.

"I want," I said "a trifle for about three pounds. A moonstone pendant or something. Yes, that's very sweet. No, I'll take it with me."

They packed it in a pretty little box for me, and I'm going to send it to Miss Middleton on the twenty-fourth. I am putting in a card with the words "From Barbara" on it. As I said, I am not giving any presents myself this year, but I do think that Barbara should repay at least some of the kindnesses which have been showered upon her so wantonly.

CHESS

(The author cannot lay claim to any great technical knowledge of chess, but he fancies that he understands the spirit of the game. He feels that, after the many poems on the Boat Race, a few bracing lines on the Inter-University Chess Match would be a welcome change.)

This is the ballad of Edward Bray,
    Captain of Catherine's, Cambridge Blue—
Oh, no one ever had just his way
    Of huffing a bishop with KB2!

The day breaks fine, and the evenings brings
    A worthy foe in the Oxford man—
A great finesser with pawns and things,
    But quick in the loose when the game began.

The board was set, and the rivals tossed
    But Fortune (alas!) was Oxford's friend.
"Tail," cried Edward, and Edward lost;
So Oxford played from the fireplace end.

We hold our breath, for the game's begun—
    Oh, who so gallant as Edward Bray!
He's taken a bishop from KQ1,
    And ruffed it—just in the Cambridge way!

Then Oxford castles his QB knight
    (He follows the old, old Oxford groove;
Though never a gambit saw the light
    That's able to cope with Edward's move).

The game went on, and the game was fast,
    Oh, Oxford huffed and his King was crowned;
The exchange was lost, and a pawn was passed,
    And under the table a knight was found!

Then Oxford chuckled; but Edward swore,
    A horrible, horrible oath swore he;

And landed him one on the QB4,
    And followed it up with an RQ3.

Time was called; with an air of pride
    Up to his feet rose Edward Bray.
"Marker, what of the score?" he cried.
    "What of the battle I've won this day?"

The score was counted; and Bray had won
    By two in honours, and four by tricks,
And half of a bishop that came undone,
    And all of a bishop on KQ6.

Then here's to Chess: and a cheer again
    For the man who fought on an April day
With never a thought of sordid gain!
    England's proud of you, Edward Bray!

PROGRESSIVE BRIDGE

There were twelve tables numbered A, B, C, up to—well, twelve of them, and I started at E, because my name is Ernest. Our host arranged us and, of course, he may have had quite another scheme in his mind. If so, it was an extraordinary coincidence that my partner's name was Ethel. She herself swore it was Millicent, but I doubt if one can trust a woman in these matters. She looked just like an Ethel. I had never seen her before, I shall never see her again, but she will always be Ethel to me.

There is only one rule at progressive bridge, and that is, if you lose you go to the next table, and if you win you stay where you are. In any case you get a fresh partner each time. That being so, it seemed hardly worth while to ask Ethel what she discarded from. As it happened, though, she began it.

"I discard from strength," she said.

"So do I," I agreed gladly. We already had a lot in common. "Great strength returns the penny," I added.

"What's that?"

"Moderate strength rings the bell. It's a sort of formula I say to myself, and brings luck. May I play to hearts?"

Ethel discarded a small heart on the first round of clubs, and a small club on the first round of hearts. After which, systematically and together, we discarded from great weakness. What with the revoke and other things they scored hundreds and thousands that game.

"You know, where providence goes wrong," I said, "is in over-estimating our skill. Providence thinks too highly of us. It thinks that if it gives us a knave and two tens between us we can get a grand slam."

"Yes; and I think—I think, perhaps, that just the least little bit it underrates Dorothy's abilities."

"Indeed?" I said. Dorothy was the person who had just taken two hundred and ninety-eight off us.

"Yes. You see Dorothy has played before, and I don't think providence knew."

"It rather looks like that."

"Mind," said Ethel graciously, "I don't blame providence for not knowing."

Dorothy laughed, and cut for me. I dealt myself three aces, and went no trumps. To my surprise Dorothy's partner doubled, and led the ace of hearts.

"One moment," I said, and I took it up, and looked at the back of it. Then I looked at the back of my own ace of hearts. Then I looked at the front of it again, and swore very softly, and played it.

"I'm very sorry," I apologised at the end of the game. "I had a wolf in sheep's clothing, an ass in a lion's skin. You saw me play the three of hearts. Well, do you know—it's very sad—he actually pretended to be the ace. Hid his head behind one card, and his feet behind another, and only—well, I thought it was the ace."

At the end of the round Ethel and I moved on.

"Good-bye," I said to Dorothy, "I like watching you play. If you wait here I shall be round again soon."

My next partner was called Aggie. Ethel addressed her as Mary, but she was much too lively for Mary. I had never seen her before, I shall never see her again, but she will always be Aggie to me.

She began at once:

"I discard from weakness, partner. I like hearts led, I never go spades on my own, I live on tapioca and toadstools, and the consequence was — —"

"It's the same with me," I said, "except about tapioca. I don't like tapioca. In fact I always—er—discard from tapioca. Otherwise we agree. It's your deal. Now," I said to Ethel, "we shall see what providence thinks of our comparative merits."

Providence made no mistake. In the whole round my partner and I scored once only. *Chicane* in spades. I moved on to G. I should never see Ethel again.

"I always play the Canadian discard," said Violet, "and I like spades led."

I need hardly say that Aggie, whom Ethel called Mary, spoke of Violet as Diana. But she looked much more like Violet, and she will always be Violet to me. I had never seen her before though, and I shall never see her again.

"So do I," I said. "Do you know Canada at all? I always wish I had been there."

"I go a good deal to Switzerland," said Violet. "Are you fond of bridge?"

"No, never; that is, I mean, 'Very.' Shall we cut?"

The "Canadian discard" hardly does itself justice under that name. It is no mere discard, but embraces all the finer points of bridge. It leads through weakness, and blocks your partner's long suits, and trumps his tricks; and, though I couldn't discover any recognised system about it, revokes now and then. I, too, from tact or sympathy, or some such motive, played the Canadian discard for all I was worth. We got to H without any difficulty....

J, K and L may be passed by, for nothing happened there. For some reason "I" was left out, or, rather, run into J. I cannot understand the point of this. To every man his table, and I feel convinced that I should have done remarkably well at "I." I had been looking forward to it all the evening. I don't much care about betting, but I am prepared to wager a hundred pounds that I should have got a grand slam at "I."

It was somewhere down in the X's that I met Maud. I had been round I don't know how many times, and was feeling quite giddy. Alice, Elizabeth, Iris, Mabel—they were all forgotten when I came to play with Maud. Hepzibah (on my right) called her Millicent or something like that, but I knew really that her name must be Maud. I had never seen her before, I shall never see her again, but she will always be Maud to me.

"I discard from hearts," I said. "I like my weakest suit led, I have revoked three times this evening, at table G on the right-hand side of the fireplace I played the 'Canadian discard,' and I shall never play it again, at K as you go round the lamp I had four aces and my partner went spades, I've had rotten luck all through, and I'm enjoying myself very much. Shall we be very cautious, or would you like to play a dashing game?"

"Oh, let's dash," said Maud.

I dealt, and went no trumps on two aces. To my great surprise Hepzibah's partner doubled and led the ace of clubs.

"One moment," I said, and I took it up and looked at the back of it. Then I looked at the back of my own ace of clubs. Then I looked at the front of it, and swore very softly, and played it.

"I'm very sorry," I began at the end of the game, "but — —"

"Haven't we met before?" said Maud, with a smile.

I looked at her hard. "By Jove! Ethel!" I cried.

"My name's Millicent," said Maud, "and seeing that we met for the first time a few hours ago— —"

"Yes, you were my first partner, 'Ethel.'"

"I'm sorry. Who is Ethel?"

"I beg your pardon," I apologised. "But I always call my first partner at progressive bridge Ethel. It's a sort of hobby with me."

"I see," said Maud—I mean Ethel. Well, I suppose I must call her Millicent now. Though I had never seen her before, and shall never see her again, she will always be Millicent to me.

DRESSING UP

I. AT A PAGEANT

Our episode is the tenth and last and (I may add unofficially) the most important. The period of it is 1750. In order to lead up to it properly it has been found necessary to start the first episode at 53 B.C. This gives the audience time to get hungry for us. "At last!" they say, when we come on, "this *is* the end, Maria."

The Duchess of Kirkcudbright (N.B.) says that they don't say that at all. They say, "Why, Henry, it's 1750! I had no idea. How the time flies when you are enjoying yourself. We *must* stay to the end; a few minutes won't make any difference now, and it's only cold mutton."

I must explain that it is the Duchess of Kirkcudbright (N.B.)—and *do* remember the "N.B.," because she is very particular about it—who in this episode condescends to dance a minuet with me: that stately old measure (if you don't trip over the sand-hill opposite Block D.) which so delighted our forefathers. It is a very sad thing, but though the whole pageant, as I have explained, hinges upon us, yet our names and description do not appear upon the programme. We are put down briefly, and I think libellously, as "Revellers." However, we learnt that we were really people of some position—right in the smart set, by all accounts; so I decided to be Lord Tunbridge Wells, and my partner the Duchess of Kirkcudbright (N.B.). That is just like her—to be a whole county, when I am only a watering-place.

We are supposed to do the "revelling" as soon as we come in. As I lead my partner down the steps I say to her, "Our revel, I think?" and she replies, "Shall we revel, or shall we sit it out?" After a little discussion we decide to revel, partly because there is nowhere to sit down, and partly because the prompter has his eye on us. Now I don't know what your idea of revelling is, but mine would include at the very least a small ginger ale and a slice of seed-cake. I mean, I don't think that would be overdoing it at all. But do you suppose we are allowed this—or indeed anything? Not likely. And yet it is just a little touch of that sort which gives verisimilitude to a whole pageant.

Before we have really got through our revelling the band strikes up, and suddenly we are all in our places for the minuet. Now, although you have paid your two guineas like a man, and are sitting in the very front row, you mustn't think we have taken all this trouble of learning the minuet simply to amuse you. Not at all. We are doing it for the sake of King George the Second, no less; a command performance. And so, when we are all in a line, just ready to start, and I whisper to my partner, "I say, I'm awfully sorry, but I've forgotten the minuet. Let's do the Lancers instead," she whispers back, "Quick! George is looking at me. Is my patch on straight?" "No," I say. "Now, don't forget you have to smile all the time. Hallo, we're off."

I am not going to describe the dance to you, because it is too difficult. But I may say briefly that there's a whole lot of things you do with your feet, and another whole lot with your hands; that you have to sway your body about in an easy and graceful manner; that you must keep one eye on the ground to see that you don't fall over the sandhills, and another eye on your partner to see that she is doing it all right, and the two of you a joint eye on everybody else to see that the affair is going symmetrically. And *then* — then comes the final instruction: "Don't look anxious. Smile, and seem to be enjoying yourself."

So far I have resisted the inclination to smile. The fact is that when I cast aside my usual habiliments and take upon me the personality of another I like to do the thing thoroughly—to enter into the spirit of the part. Now I will put the case before you, and you shall say whether I am not right.

Here we have, as I conceive the situation, a sprig of the nobility, Tunbridge Wells. He is a modest young man, who spends most of his time at his lovely Kentish seat, flanked by fine old forest trees—preferring the quiet of the country to the noise and bustle of London.

One day, however, he ventures up to town, and looking in at his customary coffee-house is hailed by an acquaintance. Tunbridge Wells, I may mention, is beautifully attired in a long blue coat, white satin waistcoat, fancy breeches, with quaint designs painted on them, silk stockings, and shoes which are too small for him.

"What are you doing to-night?" says his friend. "Come down to Chelsea with me. There's a grand Venetian *fête* on, and old George will be there."

"Right," says Tunbridge Wells.

When they get to the gardens his friend takes him aside.

"I say," he begins anxiously, "I hope you won't mind, but the fact is that I've promised you shall dance in a minuet to-night. Old George particularly wants to see one."

"But I simply couldn't," says Tunbridge Wells, in alarm. "Can't you get somebody else?"

"Oh, but you must. I've got you a jolly partner—the Duchess of Kirkcudbright (N.B.). You know the minuet, of course?"

"Well, I've learnt it; but I've very nearly forgotten it again. And my shoes are beastly uncomfortable. Before the King too! It's a bit steep, you know."

"Well then, you will. Good man."

"No, no," cries Tunbridge Wells hastily, and leads his friend aside under the trees. "I say," he begins mysteriously, "don't say anything, but— well, it's rather awkward ... I may as well tell you ... these—er—these things are a bit tight. They look all right like this, you know, but when you bend down—well, I mean I have to be jolly careful."

"I was just thinking how pretty they were. A beautiful thing, that," he adds, pointing to a crescent moon in blue on Tunbridge Wells' left knee.

"Don't touch," says Wells in alarm, "it comes off like anything. I lost a dragon-fly only yesterday. Well, you see how it is, old man. But for them I should have loved it. Only ... I say, don't be a fool.... Your servant, Duchess. I was just saying ... yes, I am devoted to it.... Yes.... Yes. Let's see, it *is* the left foot, isn't it? (Confound that idiot!)"

Now then, do you wonder that the poor fellow looks anxious, or that I feel it my duty as a good actor to look anxious too?

I have promised not to describe the whole minuet to you, but I must mention one figure in it of which I am particularly fond. In this you rejoin your partner after a long absence, and you have once more her supporting hand to hold you up. For some hours previously you have been alone in the wild and undulating open, tripping over molehills and falling down ha-has; and it is very pleasant (especially when your shoes fit you too soon) to get back to her and pour all your troubles into her sympathetic ear. It's a figure in which you stand on one foot each for a considerable time, and paw the air with the others. You preserve your balance better if you converse easily and naturally.

"I nearly came a frightful purler just now; did you see?"

"H'sh, not so loud. Have you found mother yet? She's here to-day."

"One of my patches fell off. I hope nobody heard it."

"You've got a different wig to-day. Why?"

"It's greyer. I had such a very anxious moment yesterday. You know that last bow at the end where you go down and stay under water for about five minutes? Well, I really thought—however, they didn't."

"I don't like you in this one. It doesn't suit you at all."

"So I thought at first. But if you gaze at it very earnestly for three hours, and then look up at the ceiling, you——"

"Why, there *is* mother. Hold up."

"I fancy we have rather a good action in this figure. Do you think she's noticing it? I hope she knows that we *could* stand on one leg without moving the other one at all. I mean I don't want her to think—— Hallo, here we are. Good-bye. See you again in the next figure but one." And the Duchess of Kirkcudbright (N.B.) trips off.

I put in the "N.B." because she is very particular about it; and I say "trips" because I know the ground.

II. AT A DANCE

"Then you really are coming?" said Queen Elizabeth, as she gave me my third cup of tea.

"Yes, I really am," I sighed.

"What as?"

"I don't know at all—something with a cold. I leave it to you, partner, only don't go a black suit."

"What about Richelieu?"

"I should never be able to pronounce that," I confessed. "Besides, I always think that these great scientists—I should say, philos—that is, of course, that these generals—er, which room is the encyclopædia in?"

"You might go as one of the kings of England. Which is your favourite king?"

"William and Mary. Now that *would* be an original costume. I should have——"

"Don't be ridiculous. Why not Henry VIII.?"

"Do you think I should get a lot of partners as Henry VIII.? Anyhow, I don't think it's a very becoming figure."

"But you don't wear fancy dress simply because it's becoming."

"Well, that is rather the point to settle. Are we going to enhance my natural beauty, or would you like it—er—toned down a little? Of course, I *could* go as the dog-faced man, only——"

"Very well then, if you don't like Henry, what about Edward I.?"

"But why do you want to thrust royalty on me? I'd much sooner go as Perkin Warbeck. I should wear a brown perkin—jerkin."

"Jack is going as Sir Walter Raleigh."

"Then I shall certainly touch him for a cigarette," I said, as I got up to go.

It was a week later that I met Elizabeth in Bond Street.

"Well?" she said, "have you got your things?"

"I haven't," I confessed.

"I forget who you said you were going as?"

"Somebody who had black hair," I said. "I have been thinking it over and I have come to the conclusion that I should have knocked them rather if I had had black hair—instead of curly eyes and blue hair. Can you think of anybody for me?"

Queen Elizabeth regarded me as sternly as she might have regarded—— Well, I'm not very good at history.

"Do you mean to say," she said at last, "that that is as far as you have got? Somebody who had black hair?"

"Hang it," I protested, "it's something to have been measured for the wig."

"*Have* you been measured for your wig?"

"Well—er—no—that is to say, not exactly what you might call measured. But—well, the fact is I was just going along now, only—I say, where do I get a wig?"

"You've done nothing," said Elizabeth—"absolutely nothing."

"I say, don't say that," I began nervously; "I've done an awful lot, really. I've practically got the costume. I'm going as Harold the Boy Earl, or Jessica's Last—— Hallo, there's my bus; I've got a cold, I mustn't keep it waiting. Good-bye." And I fled.

"I am going," I said, "as Julius Cæsar. He was practically bald. Think how cool that will be."

"Do you mean to say," cried Elizabeth, "that you have altered again?"

"Don't be rough with me or I shall cry. I've got an awful cold."

"Then you've no business to go as Julius Cæsar."

"I say, now you're trying to unsettle me. And I was going to-morrow to order the clothes."

"What! You haven't— —"

"I was really going this afternoon, only—only it's early closing day. Besides, I wanted to see if my cold would get better. Because if it didn't— — Look here, I'll be frank with you. I am going as Charlemagne."

"Oh!"

"Charlemagne in half-mourning, because Pepin the Short had just died. Something quiet in grey, with a stripe, I thought. Only half-mourning because he only got half the throne. By-the-way I suppose all these people wore pumps and white kid gloves all right? Yes, I thought so. I wonder if Charlemagne really had black hair. Anyhow, they can't prove he didn't, seeing when he lived. He flourished about 770, you know. As a matter of fact 770 wasn't actually his most flourishing year, because the Radicals were in power then, and land went down so. Now 771—yes. Or else as Raymond Blathwayt."

"Anyhow," I added indignantly a minute later, "I swear I'm going somehow."

"Hallo," I said cheerfully, as I ran into her Majesty in Piccadilly, "I've just been ordering—that is to say, I've been going— —I mean I'm just going to— — Let's see, it's next week, isn't it?"

For a moment Elizabeth was speechless—not at all my idea of the character.

"Now then," she said at last, "I am going to take you in hand. Will you trust yourself entirely to me?"

"To the death, your Majesty. I'm sickening for something, as it is."

"How tall are you?"

"Oh, more than that," I said quickly. "Gent's large medium, I am."

"Then, I'll order a costume for you and have it sent round. There's no need for you to be anything historical; you might be a butcher."

"Quite—blue is my colour. In fact, I can do you the best end of the neck at tenpence, madam, if you'll wait a moment while I sharpen the knife. Let's see; you like it cut on the cross, I think? Bother, they've forgotten the strop."

"Well, it may not be a butcher," said Elizabeth; "it depends what they've got."

That was a week ago. This morning I was really ill at last; had hardly any breakfast; simply couldn't look a poached egg in the yolk. A day on the sofa in a darkened room and bed at seven o'clock was my programme. And then my eye caught a great box of clothes, and I remembered that the dance was to-night. I opened the box. Perhaps dressed soberly as a black-haired butcher I could look in for an hour or two ... and— —

Help!

A yellow waistcoat, pink breeches, and—no, it's not an eider-down, it's a coat.

A yellow— — Pink br— —

I am going as Joseph.

I am going as Swan & Edgar.

I am going as the Sick Duke, by Orchardson.

I am going—yes, that's it, I am going back to bed.

AFTER DINNER

I. THE COMPLETE KITCHEN

I wat in the drawing-room after dinner with my knees together and my hands in my lap, and waited for the game to be explained to me.

"There's a pencil for you," said somebody.

"Thank you very much," I said, and put it carefully away. Evidently I had won a forfeit already. It wasn't a very good pencil though.

"Now, has everybody got pencils?" asked somebody else. "The game is called 'Furnishing a Kitchen.' It's quite easy. Will somebody think of a letter?" She turned to me. "Perhaps you'd better."

"Certainly," I said, and I immediately thought very hard of N. These thought-reading games are called different things, but they are all the same really, and I don't believe in any of them.

"Well?" said everybody.

"What? ... Yes, I have. Go on.... Oh, I beg your pardon," I said in confusion. I thought you— — N. is the letter."

"N or M?"

I smiled knowingly to myself.

"My godfather and my godmother," I went on cautiously— —

"It was N," interrupted somebody. "Now then, you've got five minutes in which to write down everything you can beginning with N. Go." And they all started to write like anything.

I took my pencil out and began to think. I know it sounds an easy game to you now, as you sit at your desk surrounded by dictionaries; but when you are squeezed on to the edge of a sofa, given a very blunt pencil and a thin piece of paper, and challenged to write in five minutes (on your knees) all the words you can think of beginning with a certain letter—well, it is another matter altogether. I thought of no end of things which started with K, or even L; I thought of "rhinoceros," which is a very long word and starts with R; but as for— —

I looked at my watch and groaned. One minute gone.

"I *must* keep calm," I said, and in a bold hand I wrote *Napoleon*. Then, after a moment's thought, I added *Nitro-glycerine*, and *Nats*.

"This is splendid," I told myself. "*Notting Hill, Nobody* and *Noon*. That makes six."

At six I stuck for two minutes. I did worse than that in fact; for I suddenly remembered that gnats were spelt with a G. However, I decided to leave them, in case nobody else remembered. And on the fourth minute I added *Non-sequitur*.

"Time!" said somebody.

"Just a moment," said everybody. They wrote down another word or two (which isn't fair) and then began to add up. "I've got thirty," said one.

"Thirty-two."

"Twenty-five."

"Good heavens," I said, "I've only got seven."

There was a shout of laughter.

"Then you'd better begin," said somebody. "Read them out."

I coughed doubtfully, and began;

"*Napoleon*."

There was another shout of laughter.

"I am afraid we can't allow that."

"Why ever not?" I asked in amazement.

"Well, you'd hardly find him in a kitchen, would you?"

I took out a handkerchief and wiped my brow. "I don't want to find him in a kitchen," I said nervously. "Why should I? As a matter of fact, he's dead. I don't see what the kitchen's got to do with it. Kitchens begin with a K."

"But the game is called 'Furnishing a Kitchen.' You have to make a list of things beginning with N which you would find in a kitchen. You understood that, didn't you?"

"Y-y-yes," I said. "Oh y-y-y-yes. Of course."

"So Napoleon——"

I pulled myself together with a great effort.

"You don't understand," I said with dignity. "The cook's name was Napoleon."

"Cooks aren't called Napoleon," said everybody.

"This one was. Carrie Napoleon. Her mistress was just as surprised at first as you were, but Carrie assured her that— —"

"No, I'm afraid we can't allow it."

"I'm sorry," I said; "I'm wrong about that. Her name was Carrie Smith. But her young man was a soldier, and she had bought a 'Life of Napoleon' for a birthday present for him. It stood on the dresser—it did, really— waiting for her next Sunday out."

"Oh! Oh, well, I suppose that is possible. Go on."

"*Gnats*," I went on nervously and hastily. "Of course I know that— —"

"Gnats are spelt with a G," they shrieked.

"These weren't. They had lost the G when they were quite young, and consequently couldn't bite at all, and cook said that— —"

"No, I'm afraid not."

"I'm sorry," I said resignedly. "I had about forty of them—on the dresser. If you won't allow any of them, it pulls me down a lot. Er—then we have Nitro-glycerine."

There was another howl of derision.

"Not at all," I said haughtily. "Cook had chapped hands very badly, and she went to the chemist's one evening for a little glycerine. The chemist was out, and his assistant—a very nervous young fellow—gave her nitro-glycerine by mistake. It stood on the dresser, it did, really."

"Well," said everybody very reluctantly, "I suppose— —"

I went on hastily:

"That's two. Then *Nobody*. Of course, you might easily find nobody in the kitchen. In fact you would pretty often, I should say. Three. The next is *Noon*. It could be noon in the kitchen as well as anywhere else. Don't be narrow-minded about that."

"All right. Go on."

"*Non-sequitur*," I said doubtfully.

"What on earth— —"

"It's a little difficult to explain, but the idea is this. At most restaurants you can get a second help of anything for half-price, and that is technically called a 'follow.' Now, if they didn't give you a follow, that would be a *Non-sequitur*.... You do see that, don't you?"

There was a deadly silence.

"Five," I said cheerfully. "The last is *Notting Hill*. I must confess," I said magnanimously, "that I am a bit doubtful whether you would actually find Notting Hill in a kitchen."

"You *don't* say so!"

"Yes. My feeling is that you would be more likely to find the kitchen in Notting Hill. On the other hand, it is just possible that, as Calais was found engraven on Mary's heart, so, supposing the cook died — — Oh, very well. Then it remains at five."

Of course you think that, as I only had five, I came out last. But you are wrong. There is a pleasing rule in this game that, if you have any word in your list which somebody else has, you cannot count it. And as all the others had the obvious things — such as a nutmeg-grater or a neck of mutton or a nomelette — my five won easily. And you will note that, if only I had been allowed to count my gnats, it would have been forty-five.

II. GETTING THE NEEDLE

He was a pale, enthusiastic young man of the name of Simms; and he held forth to us at great length about his latest hobby.

"Now I'll just show you a little experiment," he wound up; "one that I have never known to fail. First of all, I want you to hide a needle somewhere, while I am out of the room. You must stick it where it can be seen — on a chair — or on the floor if you like. Then I shall come back and find it."

"Oh, Mr Simms!" we all said.

"Now, which one of you has the strongest will?"

We pushed Jack forward. Jack is at any rate a big man.

"Very well. I shall want you to take my hand when I come in, and look steadily at the needle, concentrate all your thoughts on it. I, on the other hand, shall make my mind a perfect blank. Then your thoughts will gradually pass into my brain, and I shall feel myself as it were dragged in the direction of the needle."

"And I shall feel myself, as it were, dragged after you?" said Jack.

"Yes; you mustn't put any strain on my arm at all. Let me go just where I like, only will me to go in the right direction. Now then."

He took out his handkerchief, put it hastily back, and said: "First, I shall want to borrow a handkerchief or something."

Well, we blindfolded him, and led him out of the room. Then Muriel got a needle, which, after some discussion, was stuck into the back of the Chesterfield. Simms returned, and took Jack's left hand.

They stood there together, Jack frowning earnestly at the needle, and Simms swaying uncertainly at the knees. Suddenly his knees went in altogether, and he made a little zig-zag dash across the room, as though he were taking cover. Jack lumbered after him, instinctively bending his head too. They were brought up by the piano, which Simms struck with great force. We all laughed, and Jack apologised.

"You told me to let you go where you liked, you know," he said.

"Yes, yes," said Simms rather peevishly, "but you should have willed me not to hit the piano."

As he spoke he tripped over a small stool, and, flinging out an arm to save himself, swept two photograph frames off an occasional table.

"By Jove!" said Jack, "that's jolly good. I saw you were going to do that, and I willed that the flower vase should be spared. I'm getting on."

"I think you had better start from the door again," I suggested. "Then you can get a clear run."

They took up their original positions.

"You must think hard, please," said Simms again. "My mind is a perfect blank, and yet I can feel nothing coming."

Jack made terrible faces at the needle. Then, without warning, Simms flopped on to the floor at full length, pulling Jack after him.

"You mustn't mind if I do that," he said, getting up slowly.

"No," said Jack, dusting himself.

"I felt irresistibly compelled to go down," said Simms.

"So did I," said Jack.

"The needle is very often hidden in the floor, you see. You are sure you are looking at it?"

They were in a corner with their backs to it; and Jack, after trying in vain to get it over his right shoulder or his left, bent down and focussed it between his legs. This must have connected the current; for Simms turned right round and marched up to the needle.

"There!" he said triumphantly, taking off the bandage.

We all clapped, while Jack poured himself out a whisky. Simms turned to him.

"You have a very strong will indeed," he said, "one of the strongest I have met. Now, would one of the ladies like to try?"

"Oh, I'm sure I couldn't," said all the ladies.

"I should like to do it again," said Simms modestly. "Perhaps you, sir?"

"All right, I'll try," I said.

When Simms was outside I told them my idea.

"I'll hold the needle in my other hand," I said, "and then I can always look at it easily, and it will always be in a different place, which ought to muddle him."

We fetched him in, and he took my left hand....

"No, it's no good," he said at last, "I don't seem to get it. Let me try the other hand...."

I had no time to warn him. He clasped the other hand firmly; and, from the shriek that followed, it seemed that he got it. There ensued the "perfect blank" that he had insisted on all the evening. Then he pulled off the bandage, and showed a very angry face.

Well, we explained how accidental it was, and begged him to try again. He refused rather sulkily.

Suddenly Jack said: "I believe I could do it blindfold. Miss Muriel, will you look at the needle and see if you can will me?"

Simms bucked up a bit, and seemed keen on the idea. So Jack was blindfolded, the needle hid, and Muriel took his hand.

"Now, is your mind a perfect blank?" said Simms to Jack.

"It always is," said Jack.

"Very well, then. You ought soon to feel in a dreamy state, as though you were in another world. Miss Muriel, *you* must think only of the needle."

Jack held her hand tight, and looked most idiotically peaceful. After three minutes Simms spoke again.

"Well?" he said eagerly.

"I've got the dreamy, other-world state perfectly," said Jack, and then he gave at the knees just for the look of the thing.

"This is silly," said Muriel, trying to get her hand away.

Jack staggered violently, and gripped her hand again.

"*Please*, Miss Muriel," implored Simms. "I feel sure he is just going to do it."

Jack staggered again, sawed the air with his disengaged hand, and then turned right round and marched for the door, dragging Muriel behind him. The door slammed after them....

There is a little trick of sitting on a chair and picking a pin out of it with the teeth. I started Simms—who was all eagerness to follow the pair, and find out the mysterious force that was drawing them—upon this trick, for Jack is one of my best friends. When Jack and Muriel came back from the billiard-room, and announced that they were engaged, Simms was on his back on the floor with the chair on the top of him—explaining, for the fourth time, that if the thing had not overbalanced at the critical moment he would have secured the object. There is much to be said for this view.

BACHELOR DAYS

THE BUTTER

"You mustn't think I am afraid of my housekeeper. Not at all. I frequently meet her on the stairs, and give her some such order as "I think—if you don't mind—I might have breakfast just a *little* later—er, yes, about eight o'clock, yes, thank you." Or I ring the bell and say, "I—I—want-my-boots." We both recognise that it is mine to command and hers to obey. But in the matter of the butter I have let things slide, until the position is rapidly becoming an untenable one. Yet I doubt if a man of imagination and feeling could have acted otherwise, given the initial error. However, you shall hear.

There are two sorts of butter, salt and fresh. Now, nobody is so fond of butter as I am; but butter (as I have often told everybody) isn't butter at all unless it is salt. The other kind is merely an inferior vaseline—the sort of thing you put on the axles of locomotives. Imagine, then, my disgust, when I took my first breakfast in these rooms eleven months ago, to find that the housekeeper had provided me with a large lump of vaseline!

I hate waste in small things. Take care of the little extravagances, I say, and the big ones will take care of themselves. My first thought on viewing this pat of butter was, "It is difficult, but I will eat it." My second, "But I must tell the housekeeper to get salt butter next time."

An ordinary-minded person would have stopped there. I went one further. My third thought was this: "Housekeepers are forgetful creatures. If I tell her now, she will never remember. Obviously I had better wait until this pound is just finished and she is about to get in some more. Then will be the time to speak." So I waited; and it was here that I made my mistake. For it turned out that it was I who was the forgetful creature. And on the fifteenth day I got up to find another large pound of vaseline on my table. The next fortnight went by slowly. I kept my eye on every day, waiting for the moment to come when I could say to the housekeeper, "You will be getting me in some more butter this morning. Would you get salt, as I don't much like the other?" Wednesday came, and there was just enough left for two days. I would speak on the morrow.

But, alas! on the morrow there was another new pound waiting. I had evidently misjudged the amount.

I forget what happened after that. I fancy I must have been very busy, so that the question of butter escaped me altogether. Sometimes, too, I would go away for a few days and the old butter would be thrown away and the new butter bought, at a time when I had no opportunity of defending myself. However it was, there came a time when I had been three months in my rooms, and was still eating fresh butter; contentedly, to all appearances — in the greatest anguish of soul, as it happened. And at the end of another month I said: "Now, then, I really must do something about this."

But what *could* I do? After eating fresh butter for four months without protest I couldn't possibly tell the housekeeper that I didn't like it, and would she get salt in future. That would be too absurd. Fancy taking four months to discover a little thing like that! Nor could I pretend that, though I used to adore fresh butter, I had now grown tired of it. I hate instability of character, and I could not lend myself to any such fickleness. I put it to you that either of these courses would have shown deplorable weakness. No, an explanation with the housekeeper was by that time impossible; and if anything was to be done I must do it on my own responsibility. What about buying a pound of salt butter myself, and feeding on it in secret? True, I should have to get rid of a certain portion of fresh every day, but...

I don't know if you have ever tried to get rid of a certain portion of fresh butter every day, when you are living in a flat at the very top of chambers in London. Drop it out of the window once or twice, and it is an accident. Three times, and it is a coincidence. Four times, and the policeman on duty begins to think that there is more in it (if I may say so) than meets the eye.... But what about the fire, you will ask. Ah, yes; but I could foresee a day when there would be no fire. One has to look ahead.

Besides, as I said, I hate waste. As any cook will tell you, the whole art of housekeeping can be summed up in three words — *Watch the butter*.

More months passed and more pats of vaseline. Every day made an explanation more hopeless. I had thoughts at one time of an anonymous letter. Something in this style:

"MADAM, — One who is your friend says beware of vaseline. All is discovered. Fly before it is too late. What is it makes the sea so salt? NaCl. Sodium Chloride. THE BLACK HAND"

That would give her the impression, at any rate, that there *were* two kinds of butter. Confound it all, by what right did she assume without asking that I had a preference for fresh?

I have now been in my rooms nearly a year. Something must be done soon. My breakfasts are becoming a farce. Meals which I used to enjoy I now face as an ordeal. Is there to be no hope for me in the future?

Well, there *is* a chance? I shall have to wait until July; but with something definite in view I am content to wait.

In July I hope to go to Switzerland for a month. Two days before returning home I shall write to my housekeeper. Having announced the day of my return, and given one or two instructions, I shall refer briefly to the pleasant holiday which I have been enjoying. I shall remark perhaps on the grandeur of the mountains and the smiling beauty of the valleys, I may mention the area in square miles of the country....

And I shall dwell upon the habits of the native.

"... They live (I shall write) in extraordinary simplicity, chiefly upon the products of their farms. Their butter is the most delightful I have ever tried. It is a little salt to the taste, but after four weeks of it I begin to feel that I shall never be able to do without salt butter again! No doubt, as made in London it would be different from this, but I really think I must give it a trial. So when you are ordering the things I mentioned for me, will you ask for salt butter...."

And if that fails there remains only the one consolation. In three years my lease is up. I shall take a new flat somewhere, and on the very first day I shall have a word with the new housekeeper.

"By the way," I shall say, "about the butter...."

THE WASHING

Of course, it is quite possible to marry for love, but I suspect that a good many bachelors marry so that they may not have to bother about the washing any more. That, anyhow, will be one of the reasons with me. "I offer you," I shall say, "my hand and heart—and the washing; and, oh, *do* see that six tablecloths and my footer shorts don't get sent *every* week."

We affect Hampstead for some reason. Every week a number of shirts and things goes all the way out to Hampstead and back. I once sent a Panama to Paris to be cleaned, and for quite a year afterwards I used to lead the conversation round to travel, and then come out with, "Ah, I well remember when my Panama was in Paris...." So now, when I am asked at a dance, "Do you know Hampstead at all?" I reply, "Well, I only know it slightly myself; but my collars spend about half the year there. They are in with all the best people."

I can believe that I am not popular in Hampstead, for I give my laundress a lot of trouble. Take a little thing like handkerchiefs. My rooms, as I have mentioned, are at the very top of the building, and there is no lift. Usually I wait till I am just out into the street before I discover that I have forgotten my handkerchief. It is quite impossible to climb all the stairs again, so I go and buy one for the day. This happens about three times a week. The result is that nearly all my handkerchiefs are single ones—there are no litters of twelve, no twins even, or triplets. Now when you have a lot of strangers in a drawer like this, with no family ties (or anything) to keep them together, what wonder if they gradually drift away from each other?

My laundress does her best for them. She works a sort of birthmark in red cotton in the corner of each, so that she shall know them again. When I saw it first I was frightened. It looked like the password of some secret society.

"Are there many aliens in Hampstead?" I asked the housekeeper.

"I don't know, sir."

"Well, look here, what I found on my handkerchief. That's a secret signal of some sort, you know, that's what it is. I shall get mixed up in some kind of anarchist row before I know where I am. Will you arrange about getting my clothes washed somewhere else, please?"

"That's because you haven't got your name on it. She must mark them somehow."

"Then, why doesn't she mark them with my name? So much simpler."

"It isn't her business to mark your clothes," said the housekeeper.

That, I suppose, is true; but it seems to me that she is giving us both a lot of unnecessary trouble. Every week I pick out this decorative design with a penknife, and every week she works it in again. When you consider the time and the red cotton wasted it becomes clear that a sixpenny bottle of marking ink and a quill pen would be cheaper to her in the long run.

But she has a weakness for red cotton. The holes in the handkerchiefs she works round with it—I never quite understand why. To call my attention to them, perhaps, and to prevent me from falling through. Or else to say, "*You* did this. I only washed up to the red, so it can't be *my* fault."

If I were married and had a house of my own, there would be no man below; consequently he wouldn't wear the absurd collars he does. I get about two of them a week (so even red cotton is not infallible); and if they were the right size and a decent shape I shouldn't grumble so much. But I do object to my collars mixing in town with these extraordinary things of his. At Hampstead, it may be, they have to meet on terms of equality, more or less; force of circumstances throws them together a good deal. But in town no collar of mine could be expected to keep up the acquaintance. "You knew me in the bath," I can imagine one of his monstrosities saying; and, "When I am in the bath I shall know you again," would be the dignified reply of my "16-Golf."

Collars trouble me a good deal one way or another. Whenever I buy a new dozen, all the others seem suddenly to have become old-fashioned in shape, and of the wrong size. Nothing will induce me to wear one of them again. They get put away in boxes. Covered with dust, they lie forgotten.

Forgotten, did I say? No. The housekeeper finds them and sends them to the wash. About a month later she finds them again. She is always finding clothes which have been discarded for ever, and sending them to the wash.

The mistake is, that we have not yet come to an agreement as to what really *is* to go to the wash, and what isn't. There is a tacit understanding that everything on the floor on Monday morning is intended for Hampstead. The floor is the linen-basket. It seemed a good idea at the time, but it has its faults. Things gets on to the floor somehow, which were never meant for the north-west—blankets, and parts of a tweed suit, and sofa cushions. Things have a mysterious way of dropping. Half-a-dozen pairs of white flannel trousers dropped from a shelf one December. A pair of footer shorts used to go every week—a pair which I would carefully put down to take the bath water when I had finished with it. I wonder what those shorts thought they were doing. Probably they quite fancied themselves at football, and boasted about the goals they shot to companions whom they met at Hampstead.

"You're *always* here!" a pair of local wanderers would say.

"My dear man, I play so hard, I don't care how dirty I get."

The irony of it!

But, worst of all, the laundry-book. Every week the housekeeper says to me, "Would you pay your book now, as it's been owing for a month?" And every week I pay. That sounds absurd, but I swear it's true. Or else the weeks go very quickly.

And such amounts! Great ninepences for a counterpane or a tablecloth or a white tie. Immense numbers of handkerchiefs, counting (apparently) twelve as thirteen. Quaint hieroglyphics, which don't mean anything but seem to get added into the price. And always that little postscript, "As this has been owing for a month, we must request...."

TAKING STOCK

Beatrice has been spring-cleaning me to-day, or rather my clothes. I said, wasn't it rather early for it, as none of the birds were singing properly yet, and she had much better wait till next year; but no, she *would* do it *now*. Beatrice is my sister-in-law, and she said — — Well, I forget what she did say, but she took a whole bundle of things away with her in a cab; and I *know* John will be wearing that purple shirt of mine to-morrow. As a matter of fact, it was a perfectly new one, and I was only waiting till Lent was over.

Beatrice said the things were all lying about anyhow, and how I ever found anything to put on she didn't know; but I could have told her that they were all arranged on a symmetrical plan of my own. Beatrice doesn't understand the symmetry of a bachelor's mind. I like a collar in each drawer, and then, whatever drawer you open, there's a collar ready for you. Beatrice puts them all in one drawer, and then if you're in a hurry, and open the wrong drawer by mistake, you probably go up to the office in two waistcoats and no collar at all. That would be very awkward.

Beatrice actually wanted a braces drawer (if she hadn't married John I should never let her talk to me about braces), but I explained that I had only one pair, and was wearing those, so that it would be absurd. I expect she wanted me to think that John had two pairs. All I can say, is, that, if he has, he ought to be above taking my best shirt....

I don't think the waistcoat drawer will be a success. There are twenty-three of them, and some of them don't blend at all well. Twenty-three in one drawer—you know there are bound to be disputes. I see *William* has got to the top already. Ah! he was a fine fellow, the first I ever had. I don't quite know how to describe him, but in colour he was emerald green, with bits of red silk peeping through. Sort of open-work, you know, only where you would expect to see me there was more of *William*. I wore him at Beatrice's wedding. He *would* come. Only he wouldn't let me into the vestry. I wanted to sign my name; all the others were. I have never worn him since that day, but Beatrice has fished him out, and now he lies on the very top of the drawer.

Of course it's awfully good of Beatrice to take so much trouble about my clothes, and I'm extremely grateful, and after all she did marry my brother

John; but I think sometimes she— — Well, here's a case. You know, when you have twenty-three waistcoats you perhaps run a bit short of—of other things. So, naturally, the few you *have* got left, you— — Well, Beatrice took them all away, and said that as I couldn't possibly wear them again she'd cut them up for house-cloths. And really—half-way between winter and summer is a very awkward time for restocking. But I suppose it is going to be warmer now?

House-cloths! I bet John has a go at them first.

Beatrice found what they call in the profession a "morning-coat and vest" under the bed, and said that she would take it away and sell it for me. I like the way she "finds" things which I have been keeping for years under the bed. It is absurd to talk about "finding" anything in a small flat, because, of course, it's there all the time: but Beatrice thought that I ought to be grateful to her for the discovery, so I pretended I was. She said she would get at least half-a-crown for it; but I said I would rather have the coat. However, it turned out that I wasn't even to have had the half-crown....

I used to have thirty pairs of old white gloves in a drawer. I would take them out sometimes, and stroke them affectionately, and say, "Ah, yes, those were the ones I wore at that absolutely ripping dance when I first met Cynthia, and we had supper together. You can see where I spilt the ice pudding." Or—"This was that Hunt Ball, when I knew nobody and danced with Hildegarde all the time. She wore black; just look at them now." Well, Beatrice had *that* drawer out pretty quick. And now they are on their way to Perth or Paris, or wherever it is; except Hildegarde's pair, which will just do for the girl when she cleans the grates. I expect she really will get them you know; because John doesn't dance.

You know, you mustn't make too much fun of Beatrice; she has ripping ideas sometimes. She filled a "summer-trunk" for me—a trunk full of all the clothes I am going to want in the summer. She started with a tennis-racquet (which, strictly speaking, isn't clothes at all), and went on with some of the jolliest light waistcoats you ever saw; it made me quite hot to look at them. Well, now, that's really a good idea so far as it goes. But what will happen when the summer does come? Why, we shall have to go through the whole business all over again. And who'll arrange the winter-trunk? Beatrice. And who'll get the pink pyjamas and the green socks that there's really no room for, dear? Why, John.

Yet I am sorry for John. He was once as I am. What a life is his now. Beatrice is a dear, and I will allow no one to say a word against her, but she doesn't understand that trousers must be folded, not hung; that a collar which has once been a collar can never be opened out and turned into a cuff (supposing one wore cuffs); and that a school eleven blazer, even if it happens to be pink, must not be cut down into a dressing-jacket for the little one. Poor John! Yes, I am glad now that he has that shirt of mine. It is perhaps a *little* too bright for his complexion, perhaps he has not *quite* the air to carry it off; but I am glad that it is his. Now I think of it I have a tie and a pair of socks that would go well with it; and even *William*—can I part with *William?*—yes, he shall have *William*. Oh, I see that I must be kind to John.

Dear Beatrice! I wonder when I shall have everything straight again.

MEDES AND PERSIANS

I have already said that I am not afraid of my housekeeper, so there is no need for me to say it again. There are other motives than fear which prevent a man from arguing with housekeepers; dislike of conversation with his intellectual inferiors may be one, the sporting instinct is certainly another. If one is to play "Medes and Persians" properly, one must be a sportsman about it. Of course, I could say right out to her "Do this," and she might do it. Or she could say right out to me, "Do that," and I would reply, "Don't be absurd." But that wouldn't be the game.

As I play it, a "Mede" is a law which *she* lays down, and to which (after many a struggle) in the end I submit; a "Persian" is a law which *I* lay down, and to which ... after many a struggle ... in the end ... (when it is too late).... Well, there are many Medes, but so far I have only scored one Persian of note.

The first Mede was established last winter. For many weeks I had opened my bedroom door of a morning to find a small jug of cold water on the mat outside. The thing puzzled me. What do I want with a small jug of cold water, I asked myself, when I have quite enough in the bath as it is? Various happy thoughts occurred to me—as that it was lucky, that it collected the germs, or (who knows?) indicated a wife with five thousand a year—but it was a month before the real solution flashed across my mind. "Perhaps," I said, "it was hot once. But," I added, "it must have been a long time ago."

The discovery upset me a good deal. In the first place, it is annoying suddenly to have all one's hopes of a rich wife and protection from disease dashed to the ground; in the second, I object to anybody but a relation interfering with my moral character. Here was a comparative stranger trying to instil the habit of early rising into me by leaving shaving-water outside the door at three A.M. Was this a thing to be taken lying down?

Decidedly. So I stayed in bed and ignored the water-jug; save that each morning, as I left my rooms, I gave it a parting sneer. It was gone by the evening, but turned up again all right next day. After a month I began to get angry. My housekeeper was defying me; very well, we would see who could last the longer.

But after two months it was a Mede. Yet I have this triumph over her. That though I take the water in I ... pour it into the bath and slip back into bed again. I don't think she knows that.

Since then there have been many Medes. Little ones as to the position of the chairs; bigger ones as to the number of blankets on the bed. You mustn't think, though, that I always submit so easily. Sometimes I am firm. In the matter of "Africa Joe" I have been very firm. Here, I know, I have right on my side.

A year ago I was presented with a model of an Irish jolting car (with horse and driver complete), which had been cut out of some sort of black wood. The thing used to stand over my fireplace. Later on I acquired, at different times, a grey hippopotamus (in china) and a black elephant. These I harnessed on in front of the horse; and the whole affair made a very pretty scene, which was known to my friends as "Sunday in the Forest: Africa Joe drives his Family to Church." Besides all these I had yet another animal—a green frog climbing a cardboard ladder. I leant this against the clock. One had the illusion that the frog was climbing up in order to look at the works— which was particularly pleasing because the clock didn't go.

Very well. You have the two scenes on the same mantelboard. One, the frog as Bond Street watchmaker and jeweller, and the other (such is Empire), Africa Joe in the heart of the forest. And what does the housekeeper do? If you will believe me, she takes the frog down from the clock and props him up behind the car, just as though he were getting on to it in order to go to church with the others!

Now I do put it to you that this is simply spoiling the picture altogether. Here we have a pleasant domestic episode, such as must occur frequently in the African forests. Black Joe harnesses his horse, elephant, hippopotamus, or what not, and drives his family to the eleven o'clock service. And into this scene of rural simplicity a mere housekeeper elbows her way with irrelevant frogs and ladders!

It is a mystery to me that she cannot see how absurd her contribution is. To begin with, the family is in black (save the hippopotamus, who is in a quiet grey), so is it likely that they would tolerate the presence of a garish green-and-yellow stranger? (More than likely Joe is a churchwarden, and has not only himself to think of.) Then, again, consider the title of the scene: "Africa Joe *drives* his Family"—not "Africa Joe about to drive." The horse is trotting, the elephant has one leg uplifted, and even the hippopotamus is not in a position of rest. How then could the frog put a ladder up against a moving cart, and climb in? No; here anyhow was a Mede that must be resisted at all costs. On the question of Africa Joe I would not be dictated to.

But, after re-emphasising my position daily for three weeks, I saw that there was only one thing to do. The frog must be sacrificed to the idea of Empire. So I burnt him.

But it is time I mentioned my one Persian. It was this way. In the winter I used always to dry myself after the bath in front of my sitting-room fire. Now, I know all about refraction, and the difficulty of seeing into a room from outside, and so forth, but this particular room is unusually light, having six large windows along one of its sides. I thought it proper, therefore, to draw down the three end blinds by the fireplace; more especially as the building directly opposite belonged to the Public House Reform Association. In the fierce light that beats from reform associations one cannot be too careful.

Little things like blinds easily escape the memory, and it was obvious that it would be much pleasanter if the housekeeper could be trained always to leave the end three down. The training followed its usual course.

Every morning I found the blinds up and every morning I drew them down and left them there. After a month it seemed impossible that I could ever establish my Persian. But then she forgot somehow; and one day I woke up to find the three blinds down.

By a real stroke of genius I drew them up as soon as my dressing was over. Next morning they were down again. I bathed, dried, dressed and threw them up. She thought it was a Mede, and pulled them down.

But it was a Persian, and, as I pulled them up, I knew that I had scored.

Yet, after all, I am not so sure. For it is now the summer, and I have no fire, and I do not want the blinds left down. And when I pull them up every morning I really want to find them up next morning. But I find them down. So perhaps it really is a Mede. To tell the truth, the distinction between the two is not so clear as it ought to be. I must try to come to some arrangement with the housekeeper about it.

THE CUPBOARD

It was the landlord who first called my attention to the cupboard; I should never have noticed it myself.

"A very useful cupboard you see there," he said, "I should include that in the fixtures."

"Indeed," said I, not at all surprised; for the idea of his taking away the cupboard had not occurred to me.

"You won't find many rooms in London with a cupboard like that."

"I suppose not," I said. "Well, I'll let you have my decision in a few days. The rent with the cupboard, you say, is——" And I named the price.

"Yes, with the cupboard."

So that settled the cupboard question.

Settled it so far as it concerned him. For me it was only the beginning. In the year that followed my eyes were opened, so that I learned at last to put the right value on a cupboard. I appreciate now the power of the mind which conceived this thing, the nobility of the great heart which included it among the fixtures. And I am not ungrateful.

You may tell a newly married man by the way he talks of his garden. The pretence is that he grows things there—verbenas and hymantifilums and cinerarias, anything which sounds; but of course one knows that what he really uses it for is to bury in it things which he doesn't want. Some day I shall have a garden of my own in which to conduct funerals with the best of them; until that day I content myself with my cupboard.

It is marvellous how things lie about and accumulate. Until they are safely in the cupboard we are never quite at ease; they have so much to say outside, and they put themselves just where you want to step, and sometimes they fall on you. Yet even when I have them in the cupboard I am not without moments of regret. For later on I have to open it to introduce companions, and then the sight of some old friend saddens me with the thought of what might have been. "Oh, and I did mean to hang you up over the writing-desk," I say remorsefully.

I am thinking now of a certain picture—a large portrait of my old headmaster. It lay in a corner for months, waiting to be framed, getting more dingy and dirty every day. For the first few weeks I said to myself, "I must clean that before I send it to the shop. A piece of bread will do it." Later, "It's extraordinary how clever these picture people are. You'd think it was hopeless now, but I've no doubt, when I take it round to-morrow——"

A month after that somebody trod on it....

Now, then, I ask you—what could I do with it but put it in the cupboard? You cannot give a large photograph of a headmaster, bent across the waistcoat, to a housekeeper, and tell her that you have finished with it. Nor would a dustman make it his business to collect pedagogues along with the usual cabbage stalks. A married man would have buried it under the begonia; but having no garden....

That is my difficulty. For a bachelor in chambers who cannot bury, there should be some other consuming element than fire. In the winter I might possibly have burnt it is small quantities—Monday the head, Tuesday the watch-chain—but in the summer what does one do with it? And what does one do with the thousands of other things which have had their day—the old magazines, letters, papers, collars, chair legs, broken cups? You may say that, with the co-operation of my housekeeper, a firmer line could be adopted towards some of them. Perhaps so; but, alas! she is a willing accessory to my weakness. I fancy that once, a long time ago, she must have thrown away a priceless MS. in an old waistcoat; now she takes no risks with either. In principle it is a virtue; in practice I think I would chance it.

It is a big cupboard; you wouldn't find many rooms in London with a cupboard like that; and it is included in the fixtures. Yet in the ordinary way, I suppose, I could not go on putting things in for ever. One day, however, I discovered that a family of mice had heard of it too. At first I was horrified. Then I saw that it was all for the best; they might help me to get rid of things. In a week they had eaten three pages of a nautical almanac; interesting pages which would be of real help to a married man at sea who wished to find the latitude by means of two fixed stars, but which, to a bachelor on the fourth floor, were valueless.

The housekeeper missed the point. She went so far as to buy me an extremely patent mousetrap. It was a silly trap, because none of the mice knew how to work it, although I baited it once with a cold poached egg. It is not for us to say what our humbler brethren should like and dislike; we can only discover by trial and error. It occurred to me that, if they *did* like cold poached eggs, I should be able to keep on good terms with them, for

I generally had one over of a morning. However, it turned out that they preferred a vegetable diet—almanacs and such....

The cupboard is nearly full. I don't usually open it to visitors, but perhaps you would care to look inside for a moment?

That was once a top-hat. What do you do with your old top-hats? Ah, yes, but then I only have a housekeeper here at present.... That is a really good pair of boots, only it's too small.... All that paper over there? Manuscript.... Well, you see it *might* be valuable one day....

Broken batting glove. Brown paper—I always keep brown paper, it's useful if you're sending off a parcel. *Daily Mail* war map. Paint-pot—doesn't belong to me really, but it was left behind, and I got tired of kicking it over. Old letters—all the same handwriting, bills probably....

Ah, no, they are not bills, you mustn't look at those. (I didn't know they were there—I swear I didn't. I thought I had burnt them.) Of course I see now that she was quite right.... Yes, that was the very sweet one where she ... well, I knew even then that ... I mean I'm not complaining at all, we had a very jolly time....

Still, if it *had* been a little different—if that last letter.... Well, I might by now have had a garden of my own in which to have buried all this rubbish.

THE POST BAG

The other day I received a letter from some very old friends of mine who live in Queen Victoria Street.

Memo from Messrs Robinson, Cigar Shippers

MY DEAR SIR, — We have been very anxious at not having heard from you for nearly a year. We trust that you are in good health and that no illness or bereavement has kept you from writing to us. As you know, it is our one ambition to satisfy you in the matter of cigars, and your long silence on the subject has naturally made us apprehensive. Until we hear from you, however, we shall refuse to believe that the last lot you had from us were fatal.

Write to us frankly on the subject. How did you like the cigars we sent you last Christmas? Were they brown enough? Did they smoke to a finish strongly? One third shipper, who went to Havana especially to select this lot for you, writes us that in this respect they were fit for an ambassador or (we may add) an actor manager. What is it, then, that you are keeping back from us? Perhaps you could not light them? If this was the case you should have written to us before, and we would either have sent you others of a more porous quality or forwarded you our special gimlet, with which you could have brought about the necessary draught. Lay bare your heart to us about these cigars. Do you mind the green spots?

A connoisseur like yourself will, of course, understand that, though we guarantee that all the cigars sent out by us *can* be smoked, yet the quality of the cigar must necessarily vary with the price. This being so, perhaps you would care to try a slightly higher-priced cigar this time. We have referred to our books and we see that last year we had the pleasure of sending you a box of our famous *Flor di Cabajo* at 8s. 6d. the hundred. A nicer-coloured cigar is the *Blanco Capello* at 9s. 6d.; but we are hoping this Christmas that you will see your way to giving our celebrated *Pompadoros*, at £5 the hundred, a trial. They have all the features of the *Cabajo* which you approved, together with a breadth and charm of flavour of their own. May we send you a box of these?

Our other special lines are:

The *I am Coming*—a spirited young cigar at 7s. 6d. the hundred, of which we enclose a sample.

The *Mañana*—prompt and impressive—10s. the hundred. (*Note.*—*This cigar has a band.*)

The *There and Back*—a good persevering cigar. Only 10s. 6d. Never comes undone.

However we are quite sure that none of these will appeal to such a fastidious palate as yours must be by now, and that we may confidently rely on your order for a box of *Pompadoros*.

We may say that if you should unfortunately have completely lost your taste for cigars we shall be happy to send a box to any friend of yours. Nothing could make a more acceptable present, and nothing would endear your friend or his relatives to you so completely.

Now please write to us and tell us what you feel about it. We desire to make friends of our customers; we do not wish our business to be a mere commercial undertaking. Talk to us as freely as you would to your old college chum or fellow-clubman. We insist on being of service to you. Hoping to hear from you within a day or two, we are, etc.,

ROBINSON & Co.

I replied at once:

Memo from Me

DEAR OLD FRIEND,—A thousand thanks for your sympathetic letter, and the book with the pictures. Upon my word, I don't know which of the cigars I like best; they all look so jolly. Are they photographs or water-colours? I mean, are they really as brown as that? I like the tall, well set-up one on page 7. I see you say that it smokes strongly to a finish. That is all very well, Oswald, but what I want to know is, Does it hang the beginning at all? Some of these cigars with a strong finish are very slow forward, you know.

Many thanks for the sample. Bless you, Rupert, I didn't mind the green spots. What do they mean? That the cigar isn't quite ripe yet, I suppose. But I think you overdo the light brown spots. Or are they lucky, like those little strangers in the tea?

Yes, I think I must have some of your *Pompadoros*. Send a box at Christmas to Mr Smithson, of 199 Cornhill, with our love—yours and mine and the third shipper's. I'll pay. Not at all, Percy, it's a pleasure. He sent me some last Christmas; as it happened, I left 'em in the train before I had smoked one; but that wasn't his fault, was it? I'll get some for myself later on, if I may. You won't mind waiting?

Dear old soul, you make a mistake when you say I had some cigars from you last year. I assure you I've never heard of your name till to-day. That was why I didn't write on your birthday. You'll forgive me, won't you?

Now it is your turn to write. Tell me all about yourself, and your children, and the third shipper, and the light brown spots and everything. Good-bye! Your very loving college chum.

The correspondence concluded thus:

DEAR SIR,—We have received your esteemed order, which shall be promptly executed. Though the *Pompadoros* will not be despatched to your friend till Christmas, they are now being selected and will be put aside to cool.

We have referred again to our books and find that a box of our celebrated young *Cabajos* was indeed despatched to your address last year, on the advice of Mr Smithson, of 199 Cornhill. This was why we were so anxious at your long silence. We are, etc.,

ROBINSON & Co.

DEAR OLD SPORT,—I am afraid you misunderstood my last letter. The *Pompadoros* are for myself; it was a hundred *I am Comings* which I wanted for my friend Mr Smithson. I must tell you a funny thing about him; as a friend of both of us you will be interested. He collects cigar bands! I have no use for them myself; so, if it isn't troubling you, would you send the *Pompadoro* bands to *him*, as the *I am Comings* haven't any of their own? You might put them on the cigars to save packing. Ever your devoted fellow-clubman.

GOING OUT

Alone, I can get through an At Home with a certain amount of credit. No doubt, I make mistakes; no doubt people look at me and say: "Who is that person sitting all by himself in the corner, and keeping on eating muffins?" but at any rate I can make the function a tolerable one. When, however, I flutter in under the wing of my sister-in-law, with my hair nicely brushed and my tie pulled straight (she having held a review on the doorstep), then it is another matter altogether. It is then that I feel how necessary it is to say the right thing. Beatrice has pretty ears, but they are long-distance ones. We drifted apart immediately but I was sure she was listening.

I found myself introduced to a tall, athletic-looking girl.

"There's a great crowd, isn't there?" I said. "Can I find you some tea, or anything?"

"Oh, please," she said, with a smile.

I noted the smile, and thanked heaven that I had read my Lady Grove. In the ordinary way I say to strangers: "Will you take a dish of tea with me?" but just in time Lady Grove had warned me that this was wrong. Left to myself I hit upon the word "find." "Can I find you some tea?" It gives the idea of pursuit. And the "or anything" rounds it off well—as much as to say, "If I *should* happen to come back with a sardine on toast, don't blame *me*."

I found some tea after a long struggle, but by that time I had lost the athlete. It was a pity, because I was going to have talked to her about Surrey's victory over Kent at ladies' hockey. I don't know anything about hockey, but it's obvious that Surrey must play Kent some time, and it would be an even chance that Surrey would win. The good conversationalist takes risks cheerfully.

Well, the international having disappeared, I was going to drink the tea myself, when I caught Beatrice's eye on me.

"Will you have some tea?" I said to my neighbour.

"I think a little coffee, thank you."

"Certainly."

I pressed the tea into the hand of a retired colonel, and hurried off. Now that shows you. Alone, I should have quoted *The Lancet* on coffee microbes, and insisted on her having my cup of tea. This would have led us easily and naturally to a conversation on drinks and modern journalism. We should have become friends. I should have had an invitation from her mother to lunch; and I should have smoked two of her father's best cigars.

As it was I said "Certainly," fetched the coffee, coughed, and observed that there was rather a crowd. She said "Yes" and turned away to somebody else. Two good cigars thrown away because of Beatrice!

I was slowly recovering from my loss when Beatrice herself came up to say that she wanted to introduce me to a very nice girl called Jane something. In the ordinary way, very nice girls aren't called Jane anything, so here evidently was something exceptional. I buttoned my coat boldly, and followed her, unbuttoning it nervously on the way.

"Here he is," she said, and left us.

This is what they call introducing.

"How do you do?" I started.

"I've heard such a lot about you," began Jane brightly.

I never know what to say to that. There must be a right answer, if only Lady Grove would tell us. As it was I said "Thank you."

That felt wrong, so I added, "So have I."

"About you," I explained hurriedly. To myself I said, "You know you're not really carrying this off well. It's idle to pretend that you are."

"*What* have you heard, I wonder?" beamed Jane.

Only that her name was Jane something.

"Ah!" I said.

"Oh, you *must* tell me!"

"I mean, I've heard friends of yours mention your name."

"Oh," she said disappointedly, "I thought you meant— —"

"But, of course, everybody has heard of Jane—h'r'r'm—of Miss—er, um—I think my sister-in-law—yes, thank you, we have a train to catch, oh, must you really go?—er—good-bye."

I staggered away in pursuit of Beatrice. She dragged me up to an American girl, as I judged her.

"Here he is," she said, and passed on.

"So glad to make your acquaintance," said the American.

There *is* no answer to that, I know. I ignored it altogether, and said:

"Have you seen the Budget?"

"No. What's that?"

"Oh, you must see that."

"I will. We'll go to-morrow. Where is it?"

I don't think Americans see as much of Addison Road as they ought to. I gave the usual guide-book directions for getting there, and was just beginning to be interested when I saw Beatrice's inquiring look. "Are you behaving nicely?" it said. I passed on hastily.

I was very lonely for a while after that. Three times I got a plate of cucumber sandwiches safely into a corner, and three times a sisterly eye dragged us out again. After the third failure I saw that it was hopeless, so I wandered about and tried to decide which was the ugliest hat in the room. A man is the only possible judge in a competition of that sort. A woman lets herself be prejudiced by such facts as that it is so fashionable, or that she saw one just like it in Bond Street, my dear, at five guineas.

I had narrowed the competitors down to five, two of which were, on form, certain for a place, when I turned round and saw, in a corner behind me—

(I don't know if you will believe me)—

A man with a plate of cucumber sandwiches!

I rubbed my eyes in amazement. A man ... at an At Home ... sitting down and eating cucum— — Why, where was his sister-in-law?

There was only one thing to be done. The favourite in my competition (green, pink hoops) was disengaged for the moment. I went up to the man, took him by the arm, and dragged him away from his corner. He still held the plate in his hand, and I helped myself to a sandwich. "Must introduce you," I whispered in his ear. "Famous prize-winner." We pushed our way up to the lady.

"Here he is," I said.

And I looked round triumphantly for Beatrice.

THE SIDESMAN

(For the Third Day running)

For what seemed weeks, but was the last two days,
I'd pottered up and down that blessed baize—
Sorting out aunts in browns and aunts in greys.

For what seemed always, but was only twice
(Looking, if I may say so, rather nice),
I'd lent a hand with hymn-sheets and with rice.

Once more the dear old bells ring out; once more
I linger, pink but anxious, at the door—
This is the third time. Here she comes! Oh, lor'!

Something on these occasions goes and thrills
My fancy waistcoat at the first "I will's";
It can't be hopeless love—it must be chills.

Something—a sinking feeling—round the heart
Clutches me closely from the very start,
And tells me I am fairly in the cart.

Something.... And yet the fiercest unconcern
So masks me that the vergers never learn
How underneath my chest I yearn and yearn.

"*Wilt thou?*" And (there you are!) profoundly stirred,
A gleam of hope strikes through me—wild, absurd ...
"No luck!" I sigh. "He's on it like a bird."

"*I, Edward John*"—and lonely at the back
I wish my name were Edward; I could hack
Myself that I was never christened Jack.

"*I, Amabel* (O Amabel!) *take thee*" —
I groan, and give profoundly at the knee:
"There, but for someone else," I say, "goes Me."

Fair friends o' mine, what is it tries to shove
My heart into my watch-chain, as above?
It can't be hopeless chills, it must be love.

Yet not for Amabel. No weight of care
Clogs me as I pursue that happy pair
Into the vestry and admire them there;

Save this: I take the clergyman aside—
"Tell me," I whisper—"you're the third I've tried—
Do I, or do I not, embrace the bride?"

AN AWKWARD CASE

This is one of those really difficult cases (being the seventh of the quarter) where the editor of *The Perfect Lady* simply has to ask his readers what *A.* should have done. The sort of reply that will be given is; "*A.* should have carried it off easily." Remarks like that are unhesitatingly included among the "*Answers adjudged idiotic.*"

The thing happened in the train, while I was returning to town after a couple of nights in the country. The scene—an empty carriage, myself in one corner. On the seat opposite lay my dressing-case. I had unlocked it in order to take out a book, and was deep in this when we stopped at a wayside station. The opening of the door woke me suddenly; somebody was daring to get into my compartment. Luckily one only—a girl.

Women always wish to travel with their backs to the engine; in the event of an accident you don't have so far to go. She sat down next to my bag. Naturally I jumped up (full of politeness), seized the handle, and swung the thing up on to the rack.

That, at least, was the idea. It was carried out literally, but not figuratively. The bag went up beautifully; only—on its way it opened, and the contents showered down upon the seats, the floor, and—yes, even upon her....

The contents....

This story shows upon what small accidents great events turn. If I had only been going instead of coming back! A couple of clean shirts, a few snow-white collars, a pair of sky-blue pyjamas perfectly creased, socks and handkerchiefs neatly folded—one would not have minded all these being thrown before a stranger; at least, not so much. Going, too, the brushes and things would have been in their proper compartments; they would have swung up on to the rack. I feel convinced that, if the thing had happened going, I should have carried it off all right. We should have laughed together, we should have told each other of similar accidents which had happened to friends, and we should have then drifted into a general conversation about the weather. Going ....

But coming back! It was an early train, and I had packed hurriedly. The brushes and things had been put in anyhow, and they came out anyhow. There was an absurd piece of shaving soap wrapped up in one of "An Englishman's Letters." (I always think that things wrapped up like that look so horrible.) There was a shaving-brush in a pink piece of *Globe* lying on the sky-blue pyjamas (and the pyjamas all anyhow). Then the collars. I do think a dirty collar ... besides I had screwed them up tightly in order to get them in.... Of course she wouldn't understand that....

Socks. Now this is too awful. I don't know if I can mention this. Well— well then, they had two wretched sock-suspenders attached to them. Odd ones, as I live—black and pink. You see, I had got up in a hurry, and...

Handkerchiefs. They had been shoved into the pumps. I had been pressed for space, and...

You know, there were about thirty-nine different things that I wanted to explain to her. In novels the hero is always throwing upon the heroine an expressive glance, full of meaning. That is what I wanted. There is probably, if one only knew it, a shrug, a wave of the hand, which really does express the fact that you were coming and not going, and took in *The Times* yourself, and had packed in a hurry, and ...

If I could only have handed a Statement to the Press....

And I have yet to mention the unkindest blow of all. The evening clothes themselves, the only presentable things, stayed in the bag. If they had come out too, then I might have done something. I should have left them to the last—conspicuous upon the floor. Then I should have picked them up slowly, examined them, and nodded at the braid on the trousers as if to say, "Hang it, that's the sort of man I am really." I think, if they had come out too, I could still have carried the thing off....

What should *A.* do? Should he say to the girl, "Close your eyes and count twenty, and see what somebody's brought you," and then, while she was not looking, push the clothes under the seat? Should he be quite calm, and, stretching in front of her, say, "*My* sock, I think," or politely, "Perhaps you would care to look at a piece of *The Daily Mail*?" Should he disown the thing altogether? "I'm very sorry. Let *me* put them back for you." That would have been a master-stroke.

Or should he, to divert attention, pull the alarm, and pay his five pounds like a man?

But what *did A.* do?

Alas! He did nothing heroic. For one moment he stood there; then he pulled down the bag, fell on his knees, and began throwing the things in madly. He picked up the bag, locked it, and put it on the rack.

Then he turned to the girl. Now he was going to have spoken to her. An apology, a laugh—yes, even now he might have carried it off.

Only he happened to look up ... and he saw above her head the cord of his pyjamas dangling over the edge of the rack.

REVERIE

Dear Amaryllis,—(may I call you that?
Seeing I do not know your proper name;
And if I did, it might be something dull—
Like Madge). I offer you my broken heart,
Knowing that if you do not want the thing
You will not hesitate to mention it:
Dear Amaryllis, will you please be mine?

We met, 'twas at a dance, ten days ago;
And after sundry smiles and bows from me,
And other rather weary smiles from you,
And certain necessary calculations,
We hit at last upon the second extra,
And made an assignation for the same.
"I shall be at this corner here," you said:
And I "Right O" or words to that effect.
But when the dance came round we both were tired,
So sat it out instead beneath a palm
(Which probably was just as well for you,
And since I love you, just as well for me).
We talked, but what about I can't remember—
Save this: that you were rather keen on golf;
That I had never been to Scarborough;
And both of us thought well of Bernard Shaw.

We talked; but all the time I looked at you,
And wondered much what inspiration led
Your nose to tilt at just that perfect angle;
And wondered how on earth you did your hair;
And why your eyes were blue, when it was black;
And why—a hundred other different things.
Until at last, another dance beginning,

You left me lonely; whereupon I went
Back to the supper-room, and filled a glass
And drank, and lit a cigarette, and sighed,
And asked the waiter had he been in love,
And told the waiter, Yes, I *am* in love,
And gave him twopence, and went home to bed.

Am I in love? Well, no, I hardly think so.
For one, I'm much too happy as I am;
For two, I shall forget you by to-morrow;
For three, I do not care about your friends,
The men you danced with—bounders, all of them;
For four and five and six and all the rest,
I'm fairly sure we shall not meet again.
Not that I mind. No, as I said before,
I'm very much too happy as I am.
Besides, I shall forget you by to-morrow.

Then why this letter? Well, two incidents
Have led me to it. Here you have them both.
First, then, that sitting in my rooms last week,
Sitting and smoking, thinking—not of you,
Not altogether, but of many things,
Politics, football, dinner and tobacco—
Quite suddenly, this thought occurred to me:
"By Jove, I wish I had a little dog,
A terrier, an Irish terrier,
I wonder if the landlord would object."
And thinking thus, I rose and sighed, and bent
To take my boots off. Had a mouse appeared
I could have loved it in my loneliness.
Had but the humblest cockroach shown his head,
I think I would have said "Good-night" to it.

This too (I give it you for what it's worth):
Next morning, passing through St James's Park,
A morning for the gods, all blue and white,
I heard what, strictly, should have been a skylark,
(But, probably, was quite a common bird)
Offering up its very soul to heaven.

Then suddenly I stopped and cried, "Oh, Lord!
Oh, Lord!" I cried, "I wish it were the spring."

So there you have it. Now it's off my chest.
Just for one moment you upset me slightly,
Disturbed my usual calm serenity,
Got in my head, and set me vainly wishing
For April, and the country, and one other...
But that is over. I am whole again.
Good-bye! I shall not send this letter now.
I find I have forgotten you already.

RETROSPECT

Looking back on the past year I can see that it has been (as usual) one of noble endeavour—frequently frustrated, but invariably well meant. In accordance with the custom of the newspapers I have set down here its record of achievement in the different provinces of art, bicycling and the like; and I offer this to the public in full confidence of its sympathy and appreciation.

ART

We have had our photographs taken for the first time for many years, and if the result isn't art I don't know what is. The photographer said: "Would you like them *en silhouette* or straight-fronted?" We said in French that we had thought of *carte-de-visite*. The result is a sort of three-quarter face with one wing forward, and the man insists that we must have looked like that once. The only other achievement in the world of art is a moleskin waistcoat of some distinction. I had no idea that moles were that colour, but the man swore that when you had taken the feathers out of them you found quite a different coloured skin underneath. As he has been there and I haven't, I cannot argue with him. Altogether a good year for art.

BICYCLING

At the beginning of the year our eldest brother sold our bicycle for a sovereign and gave the sovereign to our second brother. A bad year for bicycling therefore.

SCIENCE

(I thought for the moment science began with a C, which is why it comes in here.)

Several important discoveries have been made in the year. For instance, the small white raspberries in tapioca pudding are *meant* to be there; you always thought that they had got in from some other dish, when the cook wasn't looking. And when your watch gains a foot you don't put the regulator to A because it is advancing, but to R because you want to retard it. (Or else the other way round—I have forgotten again. Anyhow, I found out that I had been doing it wrong.) Another discovery made in the early part of the year was the meaning of the phrase "Bank Rate Unchanged," but that is too technical to explain here. A record year for science.

FINANCE

The old system of keeping no accounts and never filling in the counterfoils of cheques again answered admirably.

GAMES

The past year marks an epoch in the history of games. We have retired from football and are not the cricketer we were; but, on the other hand, we have made immense strides in croquet. We improve slowly at billiards. In November we potted the red rather neatly, and everybody said, "There's no getting away from that—he *must* have meant it." As a matter of fact ... but it would spoil it to explain. In the latter part of the year we could have shown you a trick or two at tennis. That is all, except that I can no longer jump the ancestral herbaceous border, as the gardener keeps on discovering.

HYDROSTATICS

Archimedes' Principle—that if a heavy body gets into a cold bath quickly an equal amount of water gets out on to the mat quickly—was demonstrated daily, to the complete dissatisfaction of the man on the floor below, who, however, made a still more important discovery in this interesting branch of dynamics—viz. that water does not find its own level, but prefers something about ten feet lower down.

INDIGO

Indigo has maintained its *status quo* throughout the year. There have been occasions during this time when we had almost decided to be an Indigo planter in Assam rather than stick it in this beastly country. On each occasion the weather cleared just before we had packed the sandwiches.

MUSIC

Space and time alike fail us to tell of our notable triumphs upon the pianola in the year that has just elapsed. We have played the Sonata Appassionata and "Shuffling Jasper" with equal *verve* and *chiaroscuro*. The fruitness and nutty flavour of our rendering of Remorse—Valse Tzigane, No. 1,192,999, kindly return by the end of the month—will never be forgotten. In July one of the black notes stuck down and refused to budge for some time; but we got it up at last with a potted-meat opener. I say, I don't think much of Liszt. He has pace and staying power and is a good strider; quite a useful man over timber he might be; but he is a little lacking in—what shall I say, *Adagio con molto expressione ma non troppo*, if you know what I mean.

PETS

Walter, the white mouse, perished in May. The doctor said it was too much exercise on an empty—well, he put it rather crudely. You know what doctors are. And you know how white mice *will* exercise. The tailor said Walter was too small to make up into a white waistcoat, even an evening one, and that he would be hopeless as a tie. I advertised for a white mole, but they seem to be rare. Altogether it was a sad year for pets.

THOUGHT

Perhaps the past year was, above all, a year for thought. To the pursuit of thought we devoted many days in many positions. Some people would find it impossible to think properly immediately after breakfast but we proved that, given a sufficiently comfortable chair, the impossible could be achieved, that one could be as thoughtfully busy in the morning as in the afternoon.

XYLONITE

We did not do any of this.

YCLEPT

We were yclept every morning punctually at eight (and arose punctually at nine thirty) throughout the year.

ZEUGMA

I suppose you thought I couldn't do X. Y. Z. Well, this is just to show you. In the ordinary way, of course, I should have referred to the zeugma under music. We ordered a low-strung one last month, but it has not yet been delivered.

So much for my record of the past year. Reading it over now I feel that I have not spent the last twelve months in vain. At the end of them I can say truthfully that I am, if not a year wiser, at least a year older, a year fatter. And still a happy bachelor.

LETTERS TO CHARLES

I

DEAR CHARLES,—Can you lend me a penny? I have just been making up my accounts for the day (the idea occurred to me suddenly; it's a thing I have never done before) and I am seven shillings and a penny out. The seven shillings I don't mind, but the penny worries me dreadfully. I think that if you lent me another one I should gradually be able to settle down again.

I lie when I say I have never made up accounts before—I did it on one memorable occasion years and years ago. When John and I were at school we had certain expenses, such as subscriptions to the mission and to various house competitions, train fares, masters' wedding presents, haircutting and so on, which did not come out of our pocket money or tips, but which were specially sent to us from home. To save the trouble of this we were given, at the beginning of one term, five pounds to see us through all these expenses, with the understanding that we were to account for it afterwards.

"Afterwards" meant the holidays, which (to begin with) were a long way off. As they came nearer we consoled ourselves with the thought that the required "account" was a mere formality which would probably not be insisted upon; the actual money had been spent—which after all was the main thing, the idea of the whole proceeding, so to say. To wish to linger over the details of its gradual dissolution would be morbid. However to our horror a day did come in the holidays when we were peremptorily ordered to provide our account and to hand over the balance.

There is, as you know, Charles, never any difficulty about providing an account—the trouble is to hand over the balance. In our case the balance was exactly nothing, we had not a penny in our pockets. The money had been spent all right, an unusual number of masters having been married that term (some of them for the third or fourth time in the year), but we could not possibly make up our accounts so that to a farthing the two sides balanced. It would look so unnatural. How could we march solemnly into the library and say "By a perfectly amazing coincidence the money you gave us was just precisely the amount which the circumstances demanded. There is no balance."

It was a very hot afternoon, and we were unhappy. The matter of the accounts was not the only shadow which hung over us. John had a fox terrier—so had I; but whereas my dog was a Little Englander, and stayed at home, John's was an Imperialist, who roamed the country. He had disappeared again the night before, and had been observed in the morning in a village three miles away. Thither toiled John in search of him that hot afternoon, his heart torn between his love for his dog and his duty to his parents. And Rags and I remained at home to see what we could make of finance.

We made but little of it. The more I thought of it, the more impossible it seemed to say that every penny (no more, no less) of the five pounds had been spent properly. One idea I had which touched genius—namely, to furnish an account for five pounds ten (say) and point out that the balance was owing to us. Ours was always a great family for ideas. But you see the weak spot, Charles—that we hadn't demanded the ten shillings long ago.

And then John returned. No, he had not found his dog, but he had found a shilling in the road. He had spent (he simply had to spend, he said) a penny ha'penny on refreshment, but the tenpence ha'penny he had brought back joyfully. And in the evening a beautiful account (on the double-entry system) and tenpence ha'penny balance were handed over with ceremony.

So much for finance, Charles. Now I've got some news for you. *I've just had a nephew!* (Uncle doing well.) Did you know? Look here, we'll arrange a sporting match between him and your son over hurdles for 1922. Your boy will still be a year older, but, bless you, I don't mind that. My nephew is so ugly at present that I feel he must be intended for the highest honours at something. Probably hurdles. Of course if either of us perishes in the meantime the nominations become void. ("The nominations become void"—did you notice that? Quite the sportsman.)

What sort of weather are you having? I ask because the weather differs according to the locality, and down at Castle Bumpbrook it may be quite fine, while it is raining here, and *vice versa*. Why is this? Why shouldn't the weather be the same everywhere? Something to do with the solstices, I believe. What is a solstice? (I have asked you no end of questions in this letter, and I don't suppose you will answer one of them.)

Do you grow oranges at Castle? (Forgive the familiarity.) Exhausted by my divings into the remote and wicked past, I have just eaten about six. I get through quite a dozen a day. The fact is I heard a doctor say the other night that they were extremely good for the complexion—or else extremely bad, I couldn't quite catch which. He spoke very indistinctly. It was a pity that I missed what seems to have been the important word; it wouldn't have mattered so much about the "extremely." However, I go on eating them, and if one day you turn up in town and find me a full-blown mulatto, you will know that the word was "bad." I shall become a sort of test case, like "Wreford v. Partington (1883)." Eminent people will refer to me. How nice to be referred to—not that it would be the first time. "Refer to drawer," I remember on my cheques at Cambridge. That, sir, was me.

Do you know, I made up the names Wreford and Partington on the spur of the moment. The names are simple enough, but I think the combination is wonderful. There must have been such a case in 1883. Who do you think Wreford was? I fancy he was a small chandler, and he fell down the coal shoot of Partington's in Cannon Street. James Partington, the senior partner, said (fairly enough) that a great firm like his, which had branches all over England (including Norwich), must have coal some time, if they were to cope successfully with increasing foreign competition, which, owing to the present Gov— — Oh no, this was 1883; I forgot. Well, anyhow, he said they must have coal. Wreford retorted that he didn't mind their putting coal down their shoot, but when it came to including respectable citizens of London— —

You remember the excitement when the case came on? We were only babies then, but I have a recollection that my nurse was a pro-Partington. Wreford won, but as he was heavily fined for having knowingly caused a crowd to collect it did him little good, poor man.

Good-bye. Write to me soon and tell me all about Castle Bumpbrook. What a glorious name. I often say it to myself. It is the only strong language I ever use now.

II

DEAR CHARLES,—Many thanks for your definition of a solstice. Is it really? Fancy! By answering one of my questions you become a unique correspondent. Nobody else answers questions in a letter. Sometimes, of course, one is asked, "What train are you coming down by on Saturday? Let me know at once." But the proper thing to do in such a case is to wait till Saturday afternoon, and then wire "Just missed the two twenty-two. Hope to catch the next." Questions in letters are mostly rhetorical; which is why I ask you, How, oh, how could you have the nerve to head your paper "Castle Bumpbrook," and fill it with arguments against the Budget? It is hardly decent. You know, I doubt if you ought even to have heard of the Budget at Castle Bumpbrook.

What I expect from you is pleasant gossip about the miller's daughter. Is she engaged yet to the postman? Has the choir begun to practise the Christmas anthem? When does Mrs Bates' husband come out? These are the things you should tell me. Tell me, too, of your simple recreations. Has whist reached Castle Bumpbrook yet? It is a jolly game for four. One person deals and you turn up the last card, and then the— — But I must send you a book about it.

I have been having a correspondence with my landlord as to what I should do in case of fire. Of course, if your little cottage got alight, you would simply hop out of the window on to the geranium bed; but it is different in London. Particularly when you are on the top floor. Well, he tells me that I can easily get out on to Mr Podby's roof next door ... and so home. This is certainly comforting, but—Podby! I don't like it, Charles. Supposing anything happened, just think how it would look in the papers. "The unfortunate gentleman was last seen upon Mr Podby's roof...." No, I shall have to go for the drain-pipe at the back.

Look here, I have two stories to tell you. One is quite true, the other isn't. Which will you have first? All right, the truth.

When I first came to town I was very—I mean I believed everything I was told. One Sunday I met a small but elderly gentleman on the Embankment, who asked me the way to the German Embassy. He had the river to his south, so obviously all the embassies were in the other direction. I pointed vaguely towards the north. He thanked me and said that— — (By the way, do you prefer *oratio recta*? I forgot to ask you.) Well, then, he said:

"The embassies would be shut on a Sunday, hein?"

I said: "Doubtless."

He said: "I am a Professor at Heidelberg. I have just arrived in London, and I have no money. To-morrow I go to my Embassy and get some. Meanwhile, could you lend me five shillings?"

Charles, in those days I was very— — Well, I gave him half-a-crown.

He said: "I should like to pay this back to you."

I said: "Quite so. That is the idea."

"Then would you give me your card, so that I can send you the money to-morrow?"

Charles, I— — You see, I had just had some cards printed. They had "Mr" on for the first time. I was very— — Well, I gave him one.

That ends the first scene. An interval of nearly five years elapses, and we come to last Saturday. I was walking through the Green Park, when a small but elderly gentleman came up to me.

He said: "Is this the way to the School of Music?"

I said: "Which one do you want? There is the Guildhall School, and the Royal College, and the Royal Academy, and — — "

He thought for a moment, and then he said in German the German for "Do you speak German?" (My dear Charles, I *can't* spell it). I said "Nein."

He considered a little, and said, "Parlez-vous français?" I said — (What's the French for "Not very well"? Well, that's what I said).

At this his face brightened. He drew a long breath, and began:

"I am a Professor of Music at Heidelberg — — "

Charles, I had to interrupt him. I simply couldn't help it. I said; "Then you owe me half-a-crown." He stopped, and looked at me with a sort of sad dignity. Then he turned round with a sigh and plodded wearily across the park. And, oh, I do hope he had better luck with somebody else, because he has been at it for five years now, and it must be a heart-breaking life. His hair had gone quite grey since I saw him last.

Charles, you do see that that is a true story, don't you? If I had been making it up, I should have said that he gave me back my own card as a reference. I wonder why he didn't. I suppose it had got rather dirty after five years.

Do you want the other one now? It is the merest anecdote, and Hilda told it me, and I know it's not true.

She has a cat called "Didums poor little kitty wee, then"; you put the accent on the "then," and spread it out as long as you can. Well, Didums, etc., goes about eating moths; a curious diet for a cat, but I believe it keeps them thin. He swallowed them whole, you know, and Hilda told him how cruel it was. She seems to have spoken of the sufferings of the imprisoned ones in the most moving terms. Anyhow she found Didums next day up in her bedroom remorsefully eating a sealskin coat.

I am surprised at Hilda. If she is not careful her baby will grow up a journalist. I have seen him since he came back from you. This time I approached from the west, and I noticed a great difference. He is certainly a fine child, and as he let me put him to sleep I love him. After all, looks don't matter tuppence to a man. The great thing is wisdom. Knowledge comes, but wisdom lingers. I remember a General Knowledge Paper in my Mays. One of the questions was "Give a list of the chief coaling-stations you would pass on your way to New Zealand." The only two I could think of were Cyprus and Rickett Smith. I never heard whether I got full marks: probably not. But since that day knowledge has come for I have a friend in the Admiralty. He was a very high wrangler the year I wasn't, and just as Fisher is the man behind the First Lord, so he is the man behind Fisher; at least, he tells me so. And he buys his tobacco by the knot—or is it the quid?—and plays the Hague Convention at bridge, and (as I say) knows all the coaling-stations from Cambridge to New Zealand.

Wisdom Lingers. What a splendid title for a novel. You would expect a fine moral tale, and it would turn out to be the story of the Lingers family. Wisdom K. Lingers. There you have the essence of successful book-naming. I hand the idea to you, Charles, in the certainty that you would steal it anyhow.

Do you know anything about gas? I buy a lot every week for my geyser. You get about 1000 for half-a-crown. A thousand what? I don't know; but I like to take part in these great business transactions, and I am now writing to ask if they could make it 1200 seeing that I am a regular customer. No harm in asking.

III

DEAR CHARLES,—Do you truly want me to recommend you something to read? Well, why not try the serial story in some ha'penny paper? There you get a glimpse of the real thing. I turned idly to "Lepers in Israel" (or whatever it is called) last night, and found myself suddenly up to the neck in tragedy. Lord Billingham ...

Charles, you're a married man, tell me if it really is so. The gentle Pamela is urged by a cruel mother to espouse Lord Billingham for his money's sake. Lord B. is a vulgar brute, I'm afraid; in any case Pamela is all for young Prendergast; but one must be sensible, you know, and money does make a difference, doesn't it? So she becomes Lady Billingham; and a year or two later Prendergast comes back from South Africa to find that it is he who is the real Lord Billingham after all. (I got most of this from the "synopsis," which enables you to start the story now, so I can't say how it was they overlooked him in the first place.) It would be extremely cruel (you see that, Charles?) to talk about it, because Pamela would then become plain Mrs Stubbs, and no money at all; so Prendergast decides to say nothing to anybody. But he was reckoning without Mrs Trevelyan, no less. Mrs Trevelyan finds out the secret, and threatens Prendergast that she will tell everybody that he is the real Lord Billingham unless he marries her. So of course he has to.

It is at this moment that we meet Captain Pontifax. Captain Pontifax is in love with Mrs Trevelyan, at least he thinks he is, and he says that if she doesn't marry him he will let on about what happened to Mr Trevelyan, who was supposed to have died of old age. At the same time the news gets out that Prendergast is really Lord Billingham, and so Pamela does become Mrs Stubbs; and, as Prendergast cannot honourably withdraw from the alliance he is about to contract with Mrs Trevelyan, it looks as though she is going to be Lady Billingham. But on the eve of the wedding a body is found at the bottom of the old chalk quarry.... Whose? ...

What I want to hear from you, Charles, is, Do people always get married for this sort of reason? Are you really the Duke of Norfolk, and did Kitty discover your secret and threaten to disclose it? Oh, you coward! I don't mind anybody knowing that I am the true Earl Billingham.

About the body. We shall know to-morrow. I think it's Captain Pontifax myself, but I will send you a telegram.

Are you an authority on dress? A man got into my carriage on the District to-day wearing a top-hat, a frock-coat, and brown boots. Is that right? I ask it seriously, because the point I want to discover is this: Supposing you suddenly found that you had nothing in the house but brown boots and a frock-coat, would a bowler or a topper be the better way out of it?

You see the idea, Charles. If you add a bowler then the thing you have to explain away is the coat. I don't quite see how that is to be managed; you could only put it down to absent-mindedness. But if you add a topper then you have only the brown boots to account for. This could be done in a variety of ways—a foggy morning, a sudden attack of colour-blindness, or that your mother asked you to wear the thickest ones, dear, and never mind about the silly fashion. It is an interesting point which has never been dealt with properly in the etiquette-books. You and I are agreed upon the topper, it seems.

I went to a play last Tuesday. It was not bad, but the funniest scene happened right at the beginning, when I watched an American buy a seat at the box-office. They gave him J13., and he only discovered it after he had paid for it, and had put his change carefully away. Do you know, Charles, he nearly cried. The manager assured him there was nothing in it; people sat there every night, and were heard of again. It was no good. He got his money back, and went away looking quite miserable. Isn't it childish? I am going to be married on Friday, 13th May, just to show. When is that? Sickening if it's not for years and years. I have a patent calendar somewhere which tells you the date for any year up to 1928. I never know why it should stop there; something to do with the golden number getting too big. It won't go backwards either, which is a pity, because I have always wanted to know on what day of the week I was born. Nobody will tell me. It was one of the lucky days I am sure. How can I find out?

(*To-morrow.*)—I have just sent you a telegram to say that it was Sir Richard Tressider's body. Strange that you hadn't thought of him. Charles, I felt very shy in the post office. Yes, about Castle Bumpbrook. She didn't believe there was such a place; I offered to bet. We went through the Telegraph Directory together. Do you know, you come in the Castles, not in the Bumps at all. (Put me among the Bumps.) Something ought to be done about it. I always thought Castle was your Christian name, kind of.

Yes, it was Sir Richard's corpse. It occurs to me now that you will get this letter a day after the telegram. How did I put it?

"Body believed to be that of Sir Richard Tressider. Death certified as by drowning. Inspector Stockley suspects foul play."

An elevenpenny touch, Charles, and I never signed it, and you'll wonder what on earth it's all about. Probably you will dismiss it as a joke, and that would be elevenpence thrown away. That cannot be allowed. You can get a telegram repeated at half-price, can't you? I think I shall go and have a fivepenny-ha'penny repeat.

I say, what are you doing about the weather? Are you taking it lying down? I want to sign a petition, or write to my M.P. (haven't got one, then I shall write to yours), humbly showing that it's the rottenest do there's ever been. Do you remember the story (it comes in Gesta Romanorum, or should) of the man who built a model of another man and threw things at it, and the other man sat in a bath with a mirror in his hand and whenever the first man threw he ducked under the water. If he got under in time his enemy missed, and it was all right. Otherwise he was killed. Well, I am going to rig up a Negretti in my room, and throw boots at it, and if the original has to spend all his time in a cold bath ducking, I *think*, Charles, we shall get some warmer weather soon.

"Oh, how this spring of love resembleth
The uncertain glory of an April day."

Charles, in your courting days was she ever as cold to you as this?

IV

DEAR CHARLES,—Don't talk to me about politics, or the weather, or anything; I have lost my tobacco-pouch. Oh, Charles, what is to be done? It is too sad.

I bought it in a little shop at Ambleside, my first, my only friend, on the left-hand side as you go down the hill. It was descended from a brown crocodile in the male line, and a piece of indiarubber in the female; at least, I suppose so, but the man wouldn't say for certain. He called it a trade term. I smoked my first pipe from it—on the top of Scafell Pike, with all England at my feet. The ups and downs it has seen since then—the sweet-smelling briars it has met! In sickness and in sorrow it comforted me; in happiness it kept me calm. Old age came upon it slowly, beautifully. In these later years how many men have looked at it with awe; how many women have insulted it and—stitched its dear sides together!

It passed away on a Saturday, Charles; this scion of the larger Reptilia, which sprang into being among the mountain-tops, passed away in a third-class carriage at Dulwich! The irony of it! Even Denmark Hill—— But it matters not now I have lost it. Nor can I bear that another should take its place. Perhaps in a year or two ... I cannot say ... but for the present I make shift with an envelope.

Two thoughts sustain me. First, that no strange eye will recognise it as a tobacco-pouch, no strange hand (therefore) dip into it. Secondly, that the Fates, which have taken from me my dearest possession, must needs have some great happiness in store for me.

Charles, I perceive you are crying; let us turn to more cheerful things. Do you play croquet? I have just joined a croquet club (don't know why), and one of the rules is that you have to supply your own mallet. How do you do this? Of course, I know that ultimately I hand a certain sum of money to a shopman, and he gives me a very awkward parcel in exchange; but what comes before that? I have often bought a bat, and though I have not yet selected one which could make runs, I can generally find something which is pretty comfortable to carry back into the pavilion. But I have never chosen a mallet. What sort of weight should it be, and is it a good thing to say it "doesn't come up very well"? I have, they tell me, a tendency to bowness in the legs and am about a million round the biceps; I suppose all that is rather important? Perhaps they have their mallets classified for different customers, and you have only to describe yourself to them. I shall ask for a *Serviceable mallet for a blond*. "Serviceable" means that if you hit the ground very hard by accident it doesn't break; some of these highly strung mallets splinter up at once, you know. As a matter of fact, you can't miss the ball at croquet, can you? I am thinking of golf. What about having a splice with mine; is that done much? I don't want to go on to the ground looking a perfect ass with no splice, when everybody else has two or three. Croquet is a jolly game, because you don't have to worry about what sort of collar you'll wear; you just play in your ordinary things. All the same, I shall have some spikes put in my boots so as not to slip. I once took in to dinner the sister of the All England Croquet Champion. I did really. Unfortunately I didn't happen to strike her subject, and she didn't strike mine—*Butterflies*. How bitterly we shall regret that evening—which was a very jolly one all the same. Here am I, not knowing a bit how to select a mallet, and there possibly is she, having just found the egg of the Purple Emperor, labelling it in her collection as that of the Camberwell Beauty. Let this be a lesson to all of us.

Charles, I feel very silly to-night; I must be what they call "fey," which is why I ask you—How would you like to be a pedigree goat? I have just seen in an evening paper a picture of Mr Brown "with his pedigree goat." Somehow it had never occurred to me that a goat could have a pedigree; but I see now that it might be so. I think if I had to be a goat at all I should like to be a pedigree one. In a way, I suppose, every goat has a pedigree of some kind; but you would need to have a pretty distinguished one to be spoken of as a P.G. Your father, Charles, would need to have had some renown among the bearded ones; your great-uncle must have been of the blood. And if this were so, I should, in your place, insist upon being photographed as a pedigree goat "with Mr Brown." Don't stand any nonsense about that.

If I ever have a goat, and you won't let me call it Charles, I shall call it David. My eldest brother, you, know, was christened David, and called so for a year; but at the end of that time we had a boot-and-knife-boy who was unfortunately named David too. (I say "we," but I was still in the Herebefore myself.) This led to great confusion. When the nurse called for David to come and take his bottle, it was very vexing to find the other David turning up with a brown shoe in one hand and a fish-knife in the other. Something had to be done. The baby was just beginning to take notice; the leather polisher had just refused to. In the circumstances the only thing was to call the baby by his second name.

Two or three years passed rapidly, and I arrived. Just as this happened, the boot-boy took the last knife and went. Now was our chance. My second name had already been fixed; it was immediately decided that my first should be David. The new boot-boy didn't mind a bit; everybody else seemed delighted ... and then someone remembered that in ten years' time I should be going to school.

Yes, Charles, the initials D.A.M.... You know what boys are; it would have been very awkward.

And so now you see why I am going to call my pedigree goat David.

V

DEAR CHARLES,—I am learning to dance the minuet. I say "the" instead of "a" because I am sure mine is a very particular kind of one. You start off with three slides to the left, then three to the right, and then you stop and waggle the left leg. After that you bow to your partner in acknowledgement of the interest she has taken in it all, and that ends the first figure. There are lots more, but one figure at a time is my motto. At present I slide well, but I am a moderate waggler.

Why am I doing this, you ask. My dear Charles, you never know when a little thing like a minuet will turn out useful. The time may well come when you will say to yourself, "Ah, if only I had seized the opportunity of learning that when I was young, how ... etc." There were once two men who were cast ashore on a desert island. One of them had an axe, and a bag of nails, and a goat, and a box of matches, and a barrel of gunpowder, and a keg of biscuits, and a tarpaulin and some fish-hooks. The other could only dance the minuet. Years rolled by; and one day a ship put in at that island for water. As a matter of fact, there was no water there, but they found two skeletons. Which shows that in certain circumstances proficiency in the minuet is as valuable as an axe, and a bag of nails, and a goat and a box of matches, and all the other things that I mentioned just now. So I am learning in case.

My niece, aged twenty months (do I bore you?), has made her first joke: let it be put on record and handed down to those that come after. She walked into the study, where her father was reading and her mother writing. They agreed not to take any notice of her, in order to see what would happen. She marched up to her father, stroked his face, and said, "Hallo, daddy!" No answer. She gazed round; and then went over to the writing-desk. "Hallo, mummy!" Dead silence. She stood for a moment looking rather puzzled. At last she went back to her father, bent down and patted his slippers and said, "Hallo, boots!" Then she walked quite happily out of the room.

However, we won't bother about her, because I have something much more exciting to tell you. M'Gubbin has signed on for the something Rovers for next season! I saw it in the paper; it had a little paragraph all to itself. This is splendid news—I haven't been so happy about anything for a long time. Whaur's your Wully Gaukrodger now? Let us arrange a Pentathlon for them. I'll back M'G., and you can hold the towel for Gauk. My man would win at football of course, and yours at cricket, but the other three events would be exciting. Chess, golf and the minuet, I think. I can see M'Gubbin sliding—*one*, two, three, *one*, two three—there, now he's waggling his left leg. Charles, you're a goner—hand over the stakes.

Look here, I smoke too much, at least I have been lately. Let's give it up, Charles. I'll give it up altogether for a week if you will. Did you know that you can allay the craving for tobacco by the judicious use of bull's-eyes? ("Allay" is the word.) You carry a bag of bull's-eyes with you—I swear this is true, I saw it in the press—and whenever you feel a desire to smoke you just pop a bull's-eye in your mouth. In a little while, they say, your taste for tobacco—and I imagine for everything else—is quite gone. This ought to be more widely known, and then your host would say, "Try one of these bull's-eyes, won't you? I import them direct," and you would reply, "Thanks very much, but I would rather have one of my own, if I may." "Have a bull's-eye, if you like," your partner would say at a dance. Of course, too, they would have special bull's-eye compartments in trains; that would be jolly. But it would ruin the stage. The hero who always lights a cigarette before giving off his best epigram—I don't know what he'd do. You see he couldn't ... well, he'd have to wait such a time.

Why are they called bull's-eyes? I don't believe I've ever seen a bull's-eye really close. If you look a bull in the eye he doesn't go for you. Which eye? He might be a left-handed bull; you'd look at the wrong eye; then where would you be?

The world is too much with me, Charles, but all the same I've just ordered a flannel suit which will make Castle Bumpbrook stare. Sort of purplish; and it makes up very smart, and they can do me two pairs of trousers in it, whatever that means. I should have thought they could have done me as many pairs as I liked to ask for, but it seems not. They only print a limited edition, and then destroy the original plates, so that nobody else can walk about looking like me. I asked the man if he thought it would play croquet well, and he said, yes. By the way, I have learnt some more about croquet since I wrote last. First, then, you can go round in one, if you're frightfully good. I should like to go round in one; I suppose that would be the record? Secondly, if you're wired from all the balls, "so that you can't get a clear shot at every part of any one of them," you go into baulk, and have another turn. This must happen pretty often, because you could never have a clear shot at the back of a ball, unless you went right round the world the other way, and that would be too risky, besides wasting so much time. No, I can see there's a lot to learn in the game, but patience, Charles, patience. I shall go round in one yet.

VI

DEAR CHARLES,—Are you coming up to town this month? If you do we will make a journey into Shepherd's Bush together, and see the Exhibition.

I am afraid I have been doing Shepherd's Bush an injustice all these years. John and I once arranged a system of seven hells, in which we put all the men we hated. Nobody known personally to either of us was eligible (so your name never came up, dear Charles), which meant that they had to be filled with people in the public eye. The seventh division contained two only: one a socialist, who is thought a good deal of—by himself, I mean; the other a novelist who only writes about superior people who drop their "g's." The punishment for this class was simple; perpetual life in an open boat on a choppy sea, smoking Virginian cigarettes—John's idea chiefly, he being a bad sailor. The doom decreed for the unfortunates in the fifth class—now I am coming to the point of this reminiscence—was more subtle: they had to live at Shepherd's Bush, and go to a musical comedy every afternoon.

There were four men in the fifth class. Three of them we need not bother about, but the latest arrival was a certain cleric who advertised a good deal. One day we met somebody who knew him well. We broke the sad news to him gently, and he was much distressed about it. He asked if there was any hope. We replied that if his friend turned over a new leaf, and kept his name out of the papers for a bit, he might in time be promoted into the fourth division—where, every day, you watched Sussex play Essex at Leyton and had mutton sandwiches for lunch. He was so glad to hear this that he made us promise to let him know when any such step was meditated. Accordingly, after a month of perfect quiet on the part of the reverend gentleman we sent his friend a telegram: "Bernard left Shepherd's Bush by the nine o'clock steamer this morning."

And now it looks as if the Bush were much more of a place than we thought.

Every week or so I have an inspiration; and I had one yesterday, when the thought struck me suddenly that it would be a good idea to buy some postcards. You get them at the post office—six stout ones for ninepence. Oh no, that can't be right—nine stout ones for sixpence. I shouldn't think a postcard would ever get too stout—not unpleasantly so, I mean; you hardly ever see an obese postcard. I don't believe I have used one of any dimensions for ten years; yet they are such handy things when you want to say "Right O" or don't quite know whether you are "very truly" or "sincerely." The postcard touch is hereditary. Some families have it, ours hasn't. But now it is going to begin. Tomorrow I buy as many stout ones for sixpence as they will give me.

Talking of buying croquet mallets and things—I went into a little tobacconist's a little while ago (What for? Guess), and while I was there a man came in and ordered a pipe, two ounces of bird's-eye, and a box of matches. I wanted to tell him that you really required a rubber pouch as well, and a little silver thing for pressing down the tobacco. It must want some nerve to start straight off like that, especially at his age—forty or so. I am about to play golf seriously, and I shall certainly get my clubs at different shops—a driver at the Stores, a putter in Piccadilly, a niblick (what's a niblick? Anyhow, I shall have several of them, because of the name)—and several niblicks in Fleet Street. It would be too absurd to buy a dozen assorted clubs, one ball, a jersey and a little red flag all at the same place.

Yes, I should love to come down and play cricket for Castle Bumpbrook, and many thanks for asking me. I don't make runs nowadays, Charles, but if you feel that the mere presence of a gentleman from Lunnon would inspire and, as it were, give tone to the side, then I am at your service. You do say "Lunnon" in the country, don't you, when you mean London? And you say "bain't" too. How jolly! "I bain't a bowler, zur"—and you pronounce the "b-o-w" as if it were a curtsey and not a cravat. "Put Oi——" It's no good. I can't keep it up. Put me in last and I'll make 3 not out, and that will bring me top of the averages. (If you divide 3 by 0 you get an awful lot, you know.) You have an average bat, I suppose? I like them rather light—or I would take the money, whichever would be more convenient.

I have just written myself a letter, pleasantly standoffish, but not haughty. The reason is that I have my doubts about the post office, so I am giving them a test. My address, as you have discovered, is an awkward one. There are nine distinct ways of getting it wrong, and most people try two or three of them. But the letters do get here eventually, after (I expect) a good deal of sickness on the part of the postman. What I am beginning to wonder now is whether a letter with the *right* address would arrive; I fancy that the chief of the detective department would suspect a trap, and send it somewhere else; and, as I am certain that I have never received one or two letters which I ought to have had, I am writing to myself to see.

It is a great art, that of writing nicely to yourself; to say enough, yet not too much. When John was getting engaged, he wrote to himself every day. Before he started doing this he used to spend hours sitting and wondering whether the postman had been. The few letters he had had from her came by the eight-thirty post. At eight-fifteen he began to look out; nothing happened. An awful quarter of an hour followed. Eight-thirty—no postman's knock; never mind, perhaps he's late. Eight-thirty-five—well, it *is* rather a busy time; besides he may have fallen down. Eight-forty—one ray of light left; he did come once, you remember, at eight-forty-two. Eight-forty-five—despair. A half-an-hour's agony, you observe, Charles. Then he thought of writing to himself in time for that delivery. The result was that he remained quite calm, knowing that the postman was bound to come. "Ah, there he is. Will there be a letter from her? Yes—no." You see? Your heart in your mouth for five seconds only.

I never saw any of these letters. But I should say that at the beginning they were sympathetic—"Buck up, it's all right"—or hopeful—"Never mind, she'll write to-morrow"; later on they would become cynical—"Done in the eye again. What on earth do you expect?"; and, finally, I expect, insulting—"You silly ass; chuck it." ... Then, of course, she wrote.

Good-bye. Don't forget I am going to play for you. Would it be side to wear flannels? White boots would be a bit lofty, anyhow. Then I shall wear one brown pad on the right leg.

VII

DEAR CHARLES,—Many thanks for your letter. Don't side just because you get up at six o'clock, and feed the cow, or shave the goat, or whatever it is. Other people get up early too. For the last few weeks I have sprung out of bed at seven-thirty. (I always "spring" out—it is so much more classy.) But I doubt if I can keep it up.

The truth is that I have just made an unhappy discovery. I was under the impression that my man's name was Turley; I should say my third of a man, because I share with him two others, but anyhow I thought his whole name was Turley. So I used to write nice little notes, beginning, "If you're waking, call me, Turley," and leave them about for him. He invariably woke at seven and read them—and came and called me, mother dear. Of course I had to get up. Well, I have now heard that his name is really Holland, which makes all the difference. It would be absurd to write him any more notes of that kind. My one satisfaction is that I can claim to own a third of Holland, which is about 4000 square miles. Multiply that by 640 and you get it in acres. Altogether the landowner.

Moreover, Charles, my lad, you are not the one person who knows things about animals. You may be on terms of familiarity with the cow and the goat, but these are not the only beasts. What acquaintance, for example, have you with reptiles? The common newt—do you know anything about *him*? No. Well, then, now I'll tell you.

When I was seven and John was eight, we went to a naturalist's in Hampstead to inquire the price of newts. They were threepence each, not being quite in season. We bought sixpennyworth; the man put them into a paper bag for us, and we took them up on the Heath to give them a gallop. When we opened the bag we found *three* newts inside. It seemed impossible that the thing could have happened naturally, so we went back to the shop

to explain to the man that he had made a mistake. However, he hadn't; he had merely given us one newt discount. (Remember that when next you're buying them.) Well, we returned to the Heath, and they showed their paces. Now the newt is an amphibious animal (Greek); he is as much at ease in the bathroom as on the mat. So when we got them home we arranged to try them in our bath.

This is where you cry. For a time all went well. They dived, swam (back and front), trod water, returned to life when apparently drowned, and so forth. Then John pulled up the waste-pipe. He says now that he did it inadvertently, but I fancy that he wanted to see what would happen. What did happen was that they got into the whirlpool and disappeared. We turned on both the hot and cold taps to see if they would come back, but they didn't. Apparently you don't. We rushed into the garden to see if they would return by the drain-pipe with the rainwater, but not they. Only the paper bag was left to us ... and (to this day I cannot recall it without a tear) it was John who popped it.

Charles, we never saw those newts again. Crusoe, Cleaver and Robinson were their names. Robinson and Crusoe they were to have been; and when the third came, and seemed to take a fancy to Robinson, we called him Cleaver. Where are they now? In the mighty Thames somewhere, I suppose. So, Charles, if ever you are near the river, keep a friendly eye open for them, will you? They may be a little wild now, but they were good newts in their day.

We had a *Buforium* too in our time, you must know. I have just made that word up, and it means a place where you keep toads. In our case it was the sink. The toad, as you may not have realised, has no vomerine or maxillary teeth, but he *has* got a distinct tympanum. However, what I really wanted to say was that the toad has a pyriform tongue of incredible length, by means of which he catches his prey—thus differing from the frog, which leaps at 'em. We used to station a toad opposite one of the walls of the sink—of the *Buforium*—and then run his breakfast down the side. Sometimes it would be a very long centipede, and then you could have one toad for each end; or a— — What brutes little boys are; I'm not going to tell you any more about toads. (Except to say that his omosternum is generally missing. That must be very annoying.)

Did I ever talk to you about hedgehogs? We kept no end of them, but Peter was the only one who stayed. He used to live in the scullery, so as to see that no black-beetles got about. One night the cook woke up suddenly and remembered that she had left the scullery tap running. So she jumped out of bed and ran downstairs, not even stopping to put on slippers....

She was a very heavy woman.... No, Peter wasn't hurt much; but she refused to have him in the kitchen again.

This is a very zoological letter, but I just wanted to show you that you weren't the only one. Time fails me to tell you of a mole which we put in the geranium-bed, of a certain kind of caterpillar from which we caught nettlerash, of a particularly handsome triton which we kept in a tank with a crab, giving them fresh and salt water on alternative days, so that there should be no quarrelling. It is enough if I have made it clear that one does not need to have Castle Bumpbrook on one's notepaper in order to commune with nature.

I want two wedding presents—I don't mean for myself. What do you suggest? I bar anything for the table. Newly married couples might do nothing but eat to judge from the things they get given them. At present I hesitate between the useful—as, for instance, twenty thousand cubic feet of gas—and the purely ornamental—say, an antimacassar. "Mr and Mrs Samuel Jones—a towel-horse": you never see that, do you? And yet you could pay anything for a pure-bred one, and they are very useful. The bride always wears "valuable old Honiton lace, the gift of her aunt." Otherwise it's not legal. Kitty never had an aunt, had she? Then you aren't properly married, Charles. I'm sorry.

VIII

DEAR CHARLES,—A thing has just happened to me, which really only happens to people in jokes. You would not believe it did I not lay my hand on my heart—(the heart isn't on the left side, as you thought, by the way. It's bang in the middle, only the left auricle does all the work. However)—on my heart, and swear that it is true.

I was in the silver department of Liberty's buying some spoons. Yes, I fell back on spoons after all. (Never fall back on a spoon, Charles, if you can help it.) It was a hot day and the business of selection was so exhausting that I took off my hat and gloves, and laid them on a chair beside me. When it was all over the man went off to make out the bill. I wandered round the place, looking at all the other things which I wished I had bought instead. Suddenly a voice at my side said:

"Can you tell me if this is where you get ladies' jerseys for golf?"

(I told you you had to get a jersey for golf.)

I said: "Oh, do you think that is a good thing? I rather thought of spoons myself.... I mean, for a wedding present one does want something which ... Oh, I beg your pardon.... Yes, I am Mr Liberty. No liberty at all, madam,

206 | The Day's Play

I assure you.... This is the silver department, you know.... Yes, all that white shiny stuff.... Well, I daresay we could do you one, if you wouldn't mind having the lion worked on it.... No, we don't charge for the lion.... Or what about something quite simple in pewter.... Oh, I see.... The art muslin department would be the nearest thing we have ... a freer swing, certainly.... Good-morning."

Well, no, I didn't say that exactly. Having my hand on the left side of my heart it would be impossible to pretend that I did. With the best intentions in the world, how easy it is, Lucy, to slip from the rocky path of truth into the crevasse of make-believe. (Maxim from "The Fairchild Family.") But really and really, Charles, she did take me for the shopwalker in the silver department, and she did ask for ladies' golf jerseys. What I actually said was: "I'm very sorry, but I'm afraid I'm only a customer." And she said, "Oh, I'm so sorry." And then I put on my hat to show that I had one, and took it off again to show that I knew my manners, and she went off to the clock counter, and said she was sorry to trouble the man behind it, but could he tell her where she went for ladies' jerseys for golf, and he said he was very sorry, they didn't sell them, but would she like some clocks on her stockings instead. Altogether there was a good deal of sorrow going about.

But not on my part—never. In common tweeds, to be mistaken for one of those splendid frock-coated gentleman, and admitted into a lady's confidence on a question of jerseys, there was glory for you. I doubt now if I ought to have gone down to Castle Bumpbrook. Anyhow, I should have insisted on all the gate.

What was the gate? I distinctly saw three small boys hiding behind a cow. I suppose they paid all right? Charles, I did enjoy it awfully, as I think I have told you several times. It was good of you to send me in first with the postman, and as a post-man I am sure I should love him very much, but he is too fast for me on the cricket-field. There wasn't a run there, you know—a simple shot straight to cover. I expect he thought it was an express delivery or late fee stroke, with "Immediate" in the top left-hand corner; or perhaps the brown pad made him think I was a telegram. If I ever go in first with him again I shall register myself.

I gather that the vicar *has* to bowl at one end all the time, hasn't he? In lieu of tithes or something. Otherwise you get the Ecclesiastical Commissioners down on you. He varies his pitch cleverly, I admit. His firstly would take any batsman by surprise; I can't think why it only bounces once—finger-spin, I suppose. Then, immediately afterwards, you get his secondly, a high full pitch which would almost be a wide in a layman. Yet all the time you feel that he is only leading up to his sixthly and lastly, my brethren, which is one of the subtlest half-volleys I have ever seen.

Charles, I love your garden. It was jolly to see the white flower of Mrs Sinkins' blameless life again. I knew Mrs Sinkins as a bulb—I mean as a boy, and have always regarded her with affection. I suppose I shall have to wait for Dorothy Perkins. She is hardly out yet. My love is like a— — Oh, but Dorothy is pink. Anyhow, she sweetly smiles in June, and it's just on June, so I'm blowed if I don't come down to see her next month, whether you ask me or not. Better send me an invitation for form's sake.

And teach me about flowers, will you? (And I will tell you about motor omnibuses.) Why do they all end in "kins"? It can't be a coincidence that the only two which I know to talk to should do this. Funnily enough, motor omnibuses all end in Putney, which shows that this is a very small world after all, and we needs must love the highest when we see it. So near and yet so far. Doesn't it annoy you when you meet a person in London whom you last saw in Uganda, and he fatuously observes that the world is a very small place? It would have been a much smaller place, *prima facie*, if you had last seen him at Leamington.

To return to Dorothy; we have flowers in London, too. What about the Temple Show? I saw a man there with a kodak; I suppose he wanted to snap the roses as they were growing. That's the sort of weather we are on the Embankment! Oh, but the fruit there! I wish I were a prize tomato; what a complexion!